BASED ON A TRUE STORY

DANCING IN A JAR

Adele Poynter

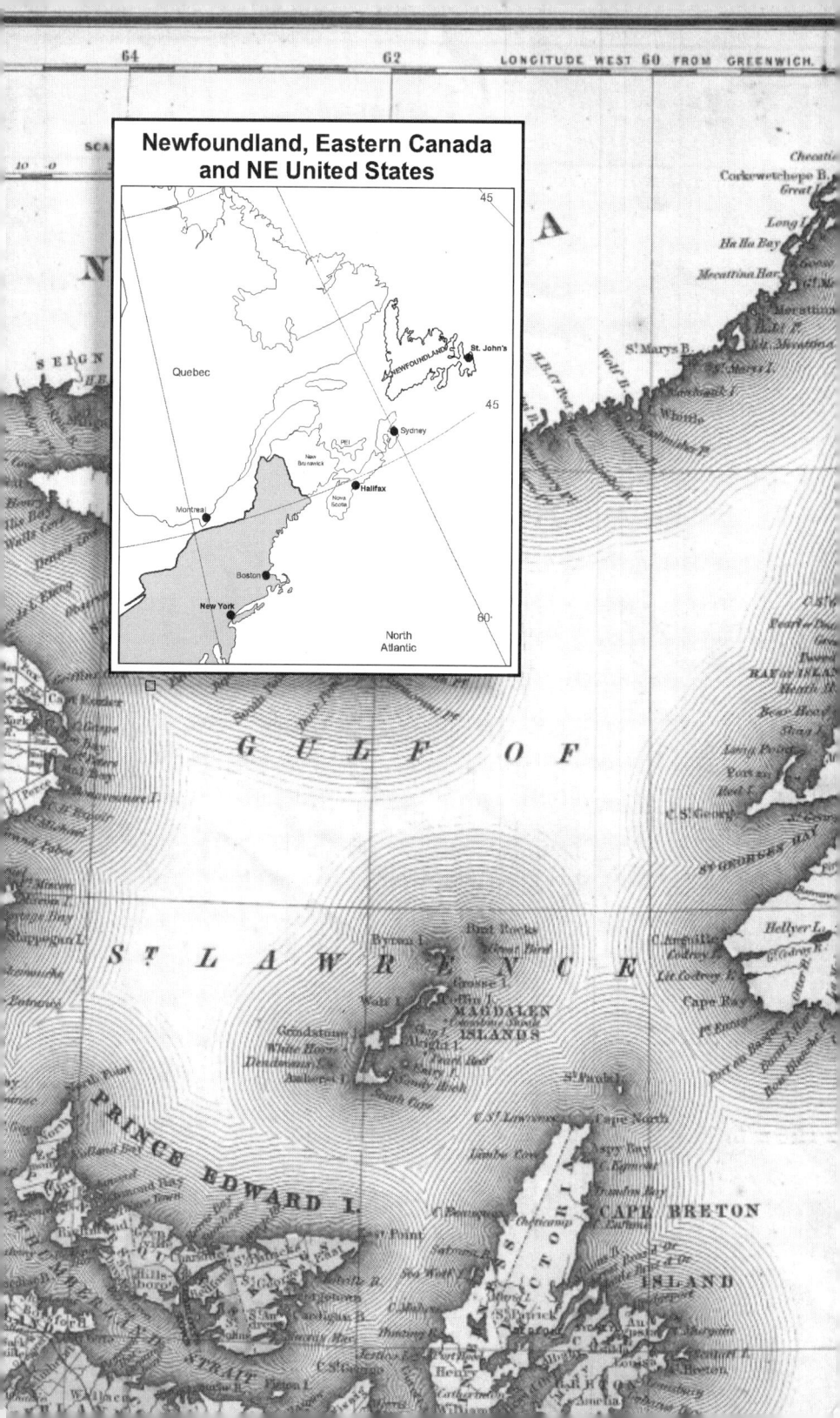

Newfoundland, Eastern Canada and NE United States

56
54
50
48
46
EW FOUNDLAND
FORTUNE BAY
PLACENTIA BAY
BONAVISTA BAY
St. Lawrence
ST. JOHN'S
French Islands
of
ST. PIERRE
et
MIQUELON
Cape Freels
Black B.
Sandy L.
Bay of Islands
L. Hooker
L. Fitz Gerald
George IV L.
Wallace L.
Wilson L.
Scott L.
Bay L.
Barrow L.
Jameson L.
Miquelon I.
C. Jervis
Indian B.
Trinity B.
Fortune L.
River of Exploits
L. Badger
Granby L.
Cow Hd.
O C E A N

FOR

Alex, Patrick, and Kate

BREAKWATER
P.O. Box 2188, St. John's, NL, Canada, A1C 6E6
WWW.BREAKWATERBOOKS.COM

A CIP catalogue record for this book is available from Library and Archives Canada.
Copyright © 2016 Adele Poynter
ISBN 978-1-55081-630-3
Map created by CeAnne Giovannini

ALL RIGHTS RESERVED. No part of this work covered by the copyright hereon may be reproduced or used in any form or by any means–graphic, electronic or mechanical—without the prior written permission of the publisher. Any request for photocopying, recording, taping or storing in an information retrieval system of any part of this book shall be directed in writing to Access Copyright, One Yonge Street, Suite 800, Toronto, Ontario, M5E 1E5.

We acknowledge the support of the Canada Council for the Arts, which last year invested $153 million to bring the arts to Canadians throughout the country. We acknowledge the financial support of the Government of Canada and the Government of Newfoundland and Labrador through the Department of Tourism, Culture and Recreation for our publishing activities.
PRINTED AND BOUND IN CANADA.

Breakwater Books is committed to choosing papers and materials for our books that help to protect our environment. To this end, this book is printed on a recycled paper that is certified by the Forest Stewardship Council˚.

She is...
a woman pressed into the shape
of a small jar, possibly attempting
to dance in there. It shows in the
way she places a seashell on a
window sill, a red-painted chair in
the corner: she is practiced in the
art of creating a still life and taking
up residence inside it.

BARBARA KINGSOLVER, THE LACUNA

ACKNOWLEDGEMENTS

This story spun around in my head for several years before I felt brave enough to start writing. Then when my own life veered from my plan, I had extra motivation to pursue the project. Friends who were writing themselves—Susan, Margo, and Deanne—provided the added incentive. My brothers Tom, Don, and Rob were very anxious to see something done with the original letters, so they provided sweet but constant pressure not to give up. Dr. John Martin made a significant contribution to understanding the full story of the St. Lawrence mines. I was so fortunate to spend time with him during his research, which helped my own understanding of a complex situation. It also allowed me the delight of spending hours with a fascinating individual.

One of my reasons for writing was to help my children get to know their grandfather at a very special time in Newfoundland history. They paid me back by helping with the typing. It is my wish this book reminds Alex, Patrick, and Kate that much of who they are comes from the people who came before them. I trust this will be the same reaction of all my nieces and nephews who read this book. I particularly hope this rings true for my sister's four sons—Don, Jack, Paul, and Jim—and will help them to better understand their complex and gifted mother.

My cousins Gemma and Betty, and my Uncle Gus all helped me to better understand St. Lawrence, then and now. My brother, Tom, years ago had dutifully audio taped some members of the Poynter and Crammond families. Those conversations helped fill in some gaps. My nephew, Don, found some more material in his mother's things and sent them along. To everyone I am truly thankful.

Sister Charlotte Fitzpatrick was a great source of knowledge on the history of the Order of the Sisters of Mercy in Newfoundland. During the writing process, I was fortunate enough to share time with my friend Dorothy who exemplifies all that is good about rural Newfoundland. My friends Maureen and Becky were instrumental in helping me prepare the manuscript to send to publishers. Unfortunately when she closes her eyes at night, I know Becky sees extra spaces, capitals where they shouldn't be, and other formatting gremlins. I'm sorry for that, but her help was instrumental. Gemma helped me sort through the final edits from the publisher who was mercifully gentle on me. I owe "you all" so much.

As always my mentor, Gretchen Bauta, inspired me in this project as in so many others.

A host of people—Mary, Tarie, Clare, Christina, Paida, and Espie as well as my doctor, Marie—all kept me comfortable and able to finish this process even as my physical abilities declined.

I'd also like to thank Rebecca Rose and James Langer for making this book a priority, and Rhonda Molloy for her beautiful design.

My husband, John, supported me as he does in everything I do. That's the beauty of being loved in precisely the right way.

PROLOGUE

I WAS ELEVEN when I discovered that my father had been married before. It's a sad reflection on the genius of us four children that it took so long to realize that our oldest sister, Barbara, was a child from a previous marriage.

Just as I tell it in this book, my father married Urla Crammond, his childhood sweetheart, in the fall of 1933 and they immediately left New York for St. Lawrence, Newfoundland. The story from my father's family was always the same: Urla went to St. Lawrence against the good judgment of the Crammonds and the Poynters. She loved Dad and did not want to be away from him. She found St. Lawrence to be an impoverished, isolated place, and she was anxious to return to the United States. She particularly did not want Barbara to grow up there. Before too long she returned to the United States and died while receiving medical care. This version of the story presents it as a tragedy not to be spoken of.

Tragedies, of course, are always intriguing. I was interested in knowing more about the story, and about my father when he was younger. My father was forty-nine years old when I was born and sixty-nine when he died. I knew him barely twenty years. I only knew his older self, whom I loved dearly, but I also loved stories about his adventurous early life and there were plenty of those.

It was a true gift, then, to come across letters from my father and Urla about their early days in St. Lawrence.

When I read them I was struck by the difference from the story we had always understood. Here were letters describing Newfoundland in a way that was not only different from the "New Jersey" perspective, but provided a fresh and surprising view of being in Newfoundland at that time. Naturally, there was poverty, tragedy, and sadness, but there was also much hope, laughter, and enterprise. Their description of the place and the landscape is a love story onto itself. Their own love story is evident on every page of each letter.

Unfortunately, there were only about fifteen letters but enough to dispel any of the notions that had come from my father's family about his Newfoundland experience. In this book, I have used direct excerpts from some of the actual letters. In other cases, I have retold their stories in my own voice. However, most of the book is a product of my own imagination. I love stories where things are not what they seem. I love that I could weave a real part of my father's life into a story I always wanted to write.

More than my father's story, however, this book tells of significant events in the development of our little country. It also includes stories of people I have known or heard about all my life and I am happy to extend the storytelling here. I mean no offense to anyone or their descendants.

As important as the story I tell is the one I didn't tell. Of all the books I thought I would write, I assumed it would be about my father's second wife, not his first. My mother was adored by everyone who knew her. In many ways, however, her story has been told in several novels set in Newfoundland. She was raised in a typical, hard-working, Catholic family without luxury. She was industrious and fun-loving, with no trouble finding joy in her life. Since I had so few letters to help me understand Urla fully, I imbued her with many of my mother's qualities. This was easy to do since they appear to be much alike, despite their very different upbringing. So my mother's story is told here too. She is also directly in the book as Florence Etchegary, a part of Urla's reading circle and an active participant in St. Lawrence life. She and my father went on to have a love story of their very own, marrying in 1947. To celebrate their wedding, my grandfather presented them with their own dairy cow, Bess.

1938

Hudson Valley Sanitarium
Montclair, New Jersey

September 20, 1938

Dear Mr. Poynter:

This is our second letter of correspondence to you concerning your late wife's affairs. We understand the post is not that reliable in your country.

Once again please accept our condolences on the passing of Mrs. Poynter.

We have assembled her personal belongings and they have been collected by your wife's sister, Mrs. William Mutch. However, in preparing a room for a new guest, the housekeeper found a large sheath of papers wedged between the mattress and bed springs. They appear to be notes of some importance to Mrs. Poynter and we thought you might like to keep them as a memento for her daughter.

We are sending you these and our heartfelt condolences on your loss.

Warm regards,
Matron Isabel Forrester

1933

The *Rosalind*
Off the coast of Eastern Canada

September 10, 1933

Dear Mom, Pop, Edith, and Howard,

Well, here it is Monday and we are still at sea after a very hectic trip. Halifax is four hours off. We didn't go up Long Island Sound as expected but put right out to sea and then north.

As I write, it is glorious out, seas are calm, and the coast of Nova Scotia is on our port. Even from here I can see the leaves have started to change, and to be sure the air has a cool nip. When the wind blows through my clothes on deck, I get some curious glances from other passengers as there are still bits of rice and confetti that fall from things I'm wearing. I am sure none of them would believe this voyage constitutes a honeymoon.

Unfortunately, we hit some poor weather around Maine. Urla took to bed yesterday at breakfast and I've yet to see her today and it's almost noon. In truth, I had totally forgotten that Urla's only experience on the water was sailing with us last year up the Hudson from Englewood. I suspect she had carried an image of us five on the *Scout*'s foredeck—enjoying the breeze with our gallant little King, his snout high on the wind, leading us on. In this case, we wouldn't be on the foredeck without being tied down, and King would be the first airborne spaniel in history.

This tub of bolts is not exactly as billed and there has been no hot water since the day we left New York. I have yet to tell Urla the *Portia* that will take us from Halifax to St. Lawrence is only half this size! But my bride is being a sport, and before this patch of rough weather, she and I played some handsome bridge with another couple on board.

George McManus is also a passenger and I have really enjoyed chatting with him. You may remember he is the creator of *Bringing up Father*.

In chats with other passengers who have been to Newfoundland, we have discovered that you may be able to bring in Christmas presents without duty and that things might not be as primitive as you might imagine.

I guess this will be all for now. More letters will follow along our rocky route.

As ever,
Donald

The Lord Nelson
Halifax, Nova Scotia

September 12, 1933

My Dear Ivah,

Not in all my life could I imagine being this sick. I prayed to God to toss me over into that furious sea—anything to get me away from the rolling and heaving of that ship. The only thing that kept me from slipping over the edge was holding to my wedding vows. Thank God I was able to keep that front and center and not let my mind run to the smell of diesel and the sharp panes of ice coming in on the wind.

I am not sure Don and I were on the same ship, as he swears the winds were balmy.

I have no idea how I will ever tell Mother that the beautiful scarf she gave me when we left Brooklyn went overboard as I heaved and the deck heaved. And I saw it go—those soft colors dropping painfully slowly in horrible contrast to the hardness all around me. I swear, I would have gone over with it if Don didn't find me and encourage me back inside. I hate for him to see me this way. I am determined to be as much an adventurer as he is and I will not let my side down. Someone pressed a cup of sweet milky tea on me and I couldn't possibly tell him, I can't abide the stuff, but somehow it did help set me right.

Don, of course, seems just fine if not positively relishing the voyage. I love watching him with his big broad smile and I can't believe he is now my husband. I have been practicing those words for five days now and I am slowly getting used to saying them without feeling churlish. No one on board the ship knows us as anything else and that is, at once, a little frightening and a little freeing. So I have been sprinkling my comments liberally with "my husband" this and "my husband" that, trying to get used to it. I think it's starting to sit better on my tongue and I hope, dear Ivah, that I haven't been boring you with the silly thoughts of a new bride. I so missed the chance to have spent some time with you after the ceremony. This all seems so brusque and unfair to you to have me marry and go away in the same breath. But I promise to write often and so must you.

We have this impossible treat of a night in a hotel here in Canada before we take our final ship to Newfoundland. Of course any bolthole would delight me as long as it wasn't heaving in the North Atlantic, but this place is almost regal in its feel. I'm just about to get ready for dinner. Don met some people on the ship and we will all dine together. He says Nova Scotia is famous for lobster although I'm not sure my stomach could handle anything other than consommé.

Please tell Mother and Daddy that everything is just fine and I will write to them from St. Lawrence.

I send you all my love, my darling sister,
Urla

P.S. Don't tell Mother about my misfortune with the scarf.
P.P.S. Give Sturdy a proper hug from me. I miss him so.

```
TELEGRAPH
US WIRELESS
TO DA POYNTER
SEPTEMBER 12 1933

C/O THE LORD NELSON
HALIFAX NOVA SCOTIA

PURCHASED SECOND HAND MACHINERY FROM SYDNEY
COAL MINE STOP WILL BE ON YOUR SHIP INTO ST
LAWRENCE STOP MEN WILL MEET YOU TO UNLOAD FULL
STOP WALTER
```

The *Portia*
Grand Bank, Newfoundland

September 15, 1933

Dear Mom and Pop,

We are almost to St. Lawrence and I thought I would send you a note from here to let you know how we are doing. I will send a more coherent affair once we settle into our boarding house.

We have had terrific storms from the time we left Halifax, waves breaking over this little ship. But the *Portia* has proven itself and we have an excellent captain at the helm. Once we reached the south coast of Newfoundland, he would heave to for periods, running into little harbors with their hidden towns. It's the most beautiful country you could ever want to see, with huge granite hills rising up from the sea, and villages tucked into little coves.

The town of Gaultois was our first stop. Urla said it looked like a fairy kingdom from one of the picture books she had as a child. The entrance is marked by a tiny lighthouse, which according to the captain is the smallest operating lighthouse in the world. The town has about fifty houses and two churches, and a curious little road made of birch logs that winds around the mountainside. This fairy kingdom even has a king. A man named Garland seems to rule the whole place and the men under him fish and cut lumber for a living. This King Garland has a beautiful three-masted schooner, which was at anchor while the King was away in his merchant boat. What a fiefdom he has! By the way, the Masonic emblem was everywhere throughout that town. The next town was Catholic, the one after that Anglican, and on it goes along the coast like a checker board.

We came upon places named Francois, Hermitage, Belloram, often making a forced landing to get out of the gale. Most of these places only have about fifty houses, but always one or two churches, and each house is painted smartly so they show up beautifully against the pines. In Hermitage, the women came down to the boat with fresh bread and raisin tea buns. The captain told me that a Mrs. Simms started it years ago and the tradition holds.

We are now in the town of Grand Bank, one of our bigger stops. Most towns have one or two schooners at anchor, but Grand Bank has six. We are coming down the coast now to flatter land and there are only two stops until St. Lawrence.

Today's sunlight has been the first we've seen since leaving home. The only cloudiness is coming from the people of this town who are very sad over the loss of two boys from the pierhead in a storm. Otherwise, everyone has been very friendly. When a boat comes in the harbor, the whole town comes down on the pier to greet it. I have learned that I must not use the word pier as that is reserved for gentlemen on sailboats! Around here everyone uses the term wharf.

Our captain has been very friendly and often comes to join mealtimes. Meals are a curious affair. The chief dish for breakfast is stew, usually with a choice of meat or veal (and meat here means beef). Of course fish is on offer three times a day and then a little before you go to bed! And fish here always means cod. Everyone holds their forks upside down. They keep both hands going all the time and it's hard not to stare as the food gets stuffed in. The coffee tastes like it was brewed for weeks at a time and the tea will pick you up and set you down with a bang. Teatime is called "mug up" and they ask you if you would like to "mug up." Urla is already filling her notebook with local expressions.

We were only ten passengers on the way up to Grand Bank, but we picked up a number of people this morning going to St. John's. We shared a good part of the south coast with a Captain Petit, known as a great "Banker," a curious term that means he owns a big fleet of fishing vessels that go to the Grand Banks. He is well traveled and is now on his way home from New York, leaving our ship at Harbour Breton. At every stop everyone seemed to know him and admire him. He was full of stories and I enjoyed time in his company, including taking a good game of cribbage from him.

The people have been welcoming and very accommodating. We have already been invited to the homes of everyone we have met. A large crowd meets every boat and there is laughter and good cheer all around even though it's clear that every community is suffering. I have never seen so many children and they come wearing clothes that look to be passed down through generations. The men all wear heavy woollen sweaters and rubber boots.

We are about to leave soon so I will give this to a steward to have mailed in Grand Bank. I hope you don't receive it before we get to St. Lawrence.

More anon,
As ever,
Donald

St. Lawrence, Newfoundland

September 16, 1933

Dear Mom and Pop,

It has taken a few days for me to settle in and put pen to paper. Hopefully this will allay any fears you may have had that Urla and I would not make it to Newfoundland. Believe me, we have arrived.

I am not sure if you have received a letter I left to be mailed from Grand Bank so I won't repeat myself too much here. The trip up was fairly smooth sailing until the final leg crossing the Gulf of St. Lawrence to the south coast of Newfoundland. It felt like my first crossing of the Atlantic to England. For Urla, it felt like a trip to the belly of the earth, but she was a good sport about it all. I am not certain she will look back on her honeymoon in the same way other gals will. But the beauty of the south coast and the kindness of the people more than made up for the waves and gales.

St. Lawrence was shrouded in fog when we rounded the cape into the harbor. For now, there is only one wharf used by some fishermen and a few government vessels, so offloading was a bit of an adventure to say the least. It appears that Siebert is behind on paying the men who have been working for him and now they refuse to work until there is some compensation. So I had to reach into my own pocket to get a few locals on the wharf to help offload the mine equipment. An invidious start.

We were met at the boat by a Mrs. Giovannini, whose boarding house is our new home for the time being. I can tell you that Urla was relieved to get on solid ground, and I was relieved to see some color return to her cheeks. I will send more news when I can. I must hurry to get this on the next boat. I imagine you will see the Crammonds at church on Sunday, so please tell them we have arrived safely and I'm sure Urla will get news to them shortly.

As ever,
Donald

St. Lawrence, Newfoundland

September 16, 1933

Dear Ivah!

I know Miss Tadmore would be upset with me using an exclamation point so carelessly in my salutation, but I am pouring out to you and it seems fitting to exclaim. Firstly, I am so happy to be writing because I never thought I would be putting pen to paper again in my life. I swear to you, dear sister, that wild horses won't drag me on to another ship. I will travel by hot air balloon or camel if I must, but it will not be again by sea. I was so sickly green when I disembarked that I fear my first impression in this town is of someone from outer space. And I felt every bit as foul as I looked.

I practically fell into the arms of our boarding house lady and she has been very kind to me. She offered to take me immediately to her house, but I did not want to be parted from Don so soon upon arrival. I have dreamed of this day for so long, and given that nothing else resembled my dream I wanted at least to be at his side. Poor Don! Not only did he have me to worry about, but there was no one to unload the machinery and I could see disappointment and frustration washing over him. I did not have the heart to add mine.

It will take some doing to square my image of a sweet rustic village with what I am afraid is the reality of St. Lawrence. But I mustn't bore you with that now and Don tells me if we don't make this postal boat you will be fretting for news.

Our boarding house is small but very tidy. We are meant to share the living area with the family, but I am much happier roosting in our own room for now. Don promises we will have our own house very soon. Tell Mother and Daddy I will write them in time for the next boat. I hope you have received my sunnier letter from Nova Scotia already.

Love from your never-setting-foot-on-a-ship sister,
U

Bucknell University
Lewisburg, Pennsylvania

September 25, 1933

Dear Urla,

Daddy brought me your letter straightaway on Sunday and I could hardly wait for them to leave to tear it open. I have missed you so much already I hardly know if I'll survive.

I am so sorry about the seasickness, but you know you hate to be on water. I hope the rest of the voyage was smooth sailing, Sis!

Bucknell is everything I remember from visiting you and more. I could lie on the rosette at the entrance to the Arts and Letters building and stare at the sky and feel the campus turn around me. I love everything about it.

My roommate's name is Vanessa Hodgeson from Gloucester, Massachusetts, and I think I like her. She is very tall and pretty and has the most delicious blonde curls—she's like someone out of a Fitzgerald novel. See! I've already started with literary references and it's my first week of class! Anyway, Mother says Vanessa is from a very old merchant family in Gloucester and seemed suitably impressed with her. I suspect by next visit Mother will be recommending I strangle my wiry black hair into soft blonde curls.

One thing for certain is that while I am busy convincing my hair to sit in a neat bob, Vanessa is already busy being "seen" by sororities. Oh Urla, dear, I wish you could be with me. I have such misgivings that Sigma Beta Phi will be interested in me as they were in you. Vanessa seems to have such a thoughtful plan for this and I am simply hoping that being Urla Crammond's baby sister will save the day and get me pledged. Mother asked me about it at least three times on Sunday. Daddy was his reassuring sweet self, but then he doesn't understand the importance of hair in a girls' world, does he?

I must run, dear U. I have to get to the library and load up on my English novels and dive in.

ADELE POYNTER

Give my new brother-in-law (see I am practising those words too!) a hug from me. I close my eyes and see you both in your little house by the sea with a rocking chair on the veranda and a new puppy by your side. Poor Sturdy is missing us both I'm afraid, but Daddy has promised extra brushings in our absence.

Sweet kisses coming your way from me,
Ivah

P.S. Your secret of the disappearing silk scarf is safe with me.
P.P.S. Let me know if you do get a puppy.
P.P.P.S. Your letter only took seven days to get to Nutley. See, you are not at the end of the earth as Granny Crammond says!

St. Lawrence, Newfoundland

September 26, 1933

Dear Viv,

Thanks so much for your letter, which arrived on Friday's mail boat. You may be impressed by it only taking five days from Halifax, but that is in CANADA, my dear. We are in a separate country altogether and I suspect our mail circumnavigates a pole before it reaches you.

I couldn't be happier that you are settling in at Bucknell. I can see the big leafy chestnuts and smell the musty dorm rooms and feel the excitement of approaching the library before anyone else in the morning. You will love it all as I did. As I still do. Don says you are to stay well away from the young engineering students, ESPECIALLY the sophomores. This is rich advice from a once sophomore who pursued a once sweet freshman, but he says this all with genuine concern not recognizing himself in any fashion. And I must second his concern: freshman can be naïve, my darling sister, so please be extra cautious.

Send me your reading list when you can. I am worried already about running out of books here. I don't see a single one in Mrs. G's house although they may be simply tucked away and I have yet to ask. I have also not visited a single other house since we arrived, as Don wants me to be careful about who I befriend until he settles things down with the men.

It appears that no one has been paid for the last month or more and poor Don has come into this situation totally blindsided. He is having trouble reaching Mr. Siebert to get the situation settled. Apparently he is duck hunting in Ohio. I would like to be hunting Siebert in Ohio! I cannot say anything to Don, but I have always had my quiet dislike of that man. But I must support my husband (see it's rolling off my tongue now). Say a little prayer that they can get paid soon. Mostly so I can get to another house and find new books.

Sweet kisses to you right back, dear Ivah,
U

```
TELEGRAPH
TO WALTER SIEBERT
SEPTEMBER 26 1933

C/O FIERCE VALLEY LODGE
ORVILLE OHIO

MEN DEMANDING PAY OWED SINCE AUGUST STOP
CANNOT PROCEED WITH PROJECT STOP PLEASE ADVISE
FULL STOP DA POYNTER
```

St. Lawrence, Newfoundland

September 27, 1933

Dear Mr. Siebert,

I hope your duck hunting was successful. I hear it's been a good season in the Midwest.

I had no response from my telegraph so I hope I have better luck reaching you by direct mail.

We have a dire situation concerning compensating the men. I would like to take a team to continue working our lease on the Black Duck property. I can't get a soul to agree until they've been paid for days worked already. They claim to not have been paid since the middle of July. As you are aware, Mr. Smith is not due back in St. Lawrence for a week or two so I am not fully informed on the situation. I am helpless to arbitrate and, despite my assurances that we will rectify this as soon as possible, to a man they refuse.

If you could wire the funds to our account in St. John's, I will take care of it from there.

In the meantime, I have been attempting to modify the machinery you purchased in Cape Breton. As you know, it was used for coal mining so some adaptation is necessary for this hard rock drilling. It is somewhat rudimentary but I feel confident that it can help us get started.

Otherwise, Urla and I are settling into our boarding house. Thank you for making those arrangements for us. It is very pleasant.

Looking forward to hearing from you shortly.

Best regards,
Don

St. Lawrence, Newfoundland

September 30, 1933

Dear Mom and Pop,

Hope this finds you both well. I was looking forward to some news from you when the coastal boat arrived yesterday, but I figure you must be busy shutting down the beach house and getting rid of pesky squirrels on Wayne Place.

It has been two weeks since our arrival and there's not much to report work wise. Looks like Siebert has fallen behind in wages and I'm having a devil of a time getting anyone to work. On top of that, he was sold a bill of goods by some fast talker in Nova Scotia and I'm stuck trying to salvage what I can from the rusty mess of machinery he has purchased. Siebert's man on site, Mr. Smith—a German geologist known here as Doc Smith—is away visiting his family until next week, so I am in the dark. At least the typewriter I bought in Halifax is serving me well.

Urla and I are settled into the boarding house. It is one of the loveliest houses in town. We couldn't ask for better people to take care of us, but I will be happy to get in our own place as will Urla. I had better wait until I get the men paid before I remind Siebert about that promise. Pop, if you could, please check my bank account when you're next in the city. I should have a deposit from Siebert on the middle of each month.

Your son,
Donald

24 Wayne Place
Nutley, New Jersey

October 6, 1933

Dear Donald,

Your letter arrived yesterday and we are both encouraged to get a quick response back to you. Thank you for the letter and most particularly the beautiful stamps. They make a handsome addition to my collection and the beauty of the Newfoundland designs seems to be well known by some serious collectors I've met in the city.

I hope by now you have heard from Siebert. I realize you have had an inauspicious start but I caution you that times everywhere are tough. *The New York Times* ran an article on Friday about mines in Mexico and mentioned fluorspar. I would suggest not doing anything to make Siebert move his money south rather than north. Do not forget that in '29 lots of people worked for nothing and felt blessed to have a job to hold onto. You may want to remind the men of St. Lawrence about American fortitude.

Yes, we have closed down the house at Oak Beach for another year. I put the old buggy in the garage after a very short season but as I say, times are tough and I limited my gasoline use in line with your mother's horsewhip on our household accounts.

Speaking of accounts, I will check on yours when next in NYC. Nevertheless, I think your worry is misplaced as I feel confident that Siebert is a man of his word.

I am enclosing an article from *The Times*, Saturday past edition. They ran a two-page spread on collectible art and craft in the city. Hopefully you can see from the piece that our ARHEPO Gifts earned fourth place in their competition. We were all thrilled. I submitted one of my recent designs with a wrought-iron base carved to look like a sextant, and the lampshade fashioned as a sail heading downwind. I have received three commissions already based on that article. However, that will not keep my eighteen people fully employed and the market really is tightening up. The biggest challenge is getting credit from the banks. I feel people want to spend but the banks are tight as a clam. Mother thinks I should let go the sales people and go on the road myself as an artist selling his own product. I am not sure of this but I will keep you posted. For now, we have enough work on the books to get the whole company through February.

I notice you are boarding with Italians. Do you remember the DeNilos (you kids used to call them "de tomatoes") who lived on the corner of Wayne Place and Passaic Avenue? They moved to the city about six years ago and it might not have been a good idea. We just heard that Paul DeNilo, the father, was killed in a mob style shooting in Queens. So watch your back!

Love,
Pop

Donald Dear,

I'll include a quick hello with Pop's. So happy you and Urla are settled in. I did see the Crammonds. I wish Mrs. C would stop looking as though you have taken her precious child to Outer Mongolia. But for your sake I am on my best behavior.

I know you mentioned to Pop about your bank account. I'm hoping you remember your promise to pay for Edith's singing lessons. The City Opera is showing such interest in her and I would hate to cut short her progress. Pop would never agree to such frivolous spending unless it's on himself of course. Thank you darling for your generous offer.

I see the name of your landlady is Giovannini. Is there nowhere those Catholic Italians haven't gone?

Love to you and your bride,
Mother

St. Lawrence, Newfoundland
October 6, 1933

Dear Ivah,

Don was home for lunch today and told me the mail boat will be leaving in a couple of hours because of some looming bad weather, so I am sending you a quick note for fear that you will think I've dropped off the earth.

Remember I told you that I hadn't gone into another house except Mrs. Giovannini's? Well this week I had such extreme cabin fever I just had to get outside for a long walk. I miscalculated on the weather—easy to do here as it changes every five minutes. Just as it was starting to rain, I bumped into Mrs. Giovannini going to her neighbor's house and she encouraged me along for a visit.

Oh dear Viv, it is slowly dawning on me that we are staying in one of the nicest houses in the town. I feel so totally silly for not having taken in my surroundings a little more fully before this. Now I see how many houses are badly in need of a coat of paint. And even when that is not the case, the outside still belies the struggles within.

Mrs. G's neighbor's name is Mrs. Edwards, and her house is really just two big rooms and what looks like a rabbit warren of bedrooms in behind. We sat in the kitchen which contained a big stove, a bigger table and BIG group of children. There was only one cupboard and when Mrs. Edwards opened it to get molasses for our tea it reminded me of looking at dollhouse groceries. There was one bag of sugar, one bottle of molasses, one box of tea, and the like. The kitchen table was buried under a dozen loaves of bread, still in their baking tins, and around it a number of birdlike beaks waiting to be fed. I have never seen so much bread anywhere except in Finister's bakery at home. I can also guarantee that all that bread would never have a chance to go dry because I watched it being devoured right in front of me as a mess of little hands and those bird beaks finished off the works. It was straight out of a Dickens novel.

Just as I was recovering from that, I saw a movement in the corner and nearly dropped my teacup from fright. There on a long wooden couch was her husband, asleep amidst all the slurping and eating and conversation. But all I could see was scraps of hair here and there and elfin ears and a furry mouth emitting a low growl. Of course the two women doubled over in laughter at my fright and I'm sure I'll be the talk of the town in a matter of hours. Mrs. G said, "Sure, my honey, it's just Joe having a kip before tea." That roughly translates as "It's Mr. Edwards having a small nap before dinner." Apparently, sleeping in your kitchen on a "daybed" is all the rage in St. Lawrence!

I realize I have to get out more and visit if I'm going to adapt at all. I'm equal parts nervous and worried about the gap between my expectations and reality. I really have no experience to help me set my sails for this place.

I'd be much happier sitting next to you in class. Oh well, I have a few good books to bury myself in and our boarding house is warm and cozy, so I have no complaints. *Poor Don is still trying to get some resolution with the men so work can continue. I think he is slowly seeing he has been blindsided by Siebert, but he doesn't acknowledge it and I don't either. Best to carry on so everything is according to plan. Maybe this is what marriage is meant to be. I sure hope not.*

Love,
Urla

St. Lawrence Corporation Ltd.
Room 1116, 120 Broadway
New York 5, NY

October 6, 1933

Dear Don,

I received your telegraph followed by your letter in due course. I did not respond immediately as frankly there is no immediate response. I am admittedly behind in my payments to the men and I don't see this situation improving until we raise some more capital at this end, which I am intent on doing.

I am working with John Whitman who is helping open doors for me here in the city. As you can imagine, this is a tough sell, but I am confident we can bankroll next year's work with some luck on our side.

In the interim, I would ask you to approach some of the shopkeepers in town to see if they would extend credit to our men until I can settle up when this next round of funding is secured. This is common practice in that neck of the woods as the fish merchants have done it for years. You should have no problem in arranging this.

We need to keep the focus on getting 2,000 tons of spar on the wharf by spring. If it suits DOSCO's needs then we are in business.

Good to hear that the Nova Scotia machinery will work out for us. Some positive results from Black Duck will help me close the deal at this end. So let's encourage everyone to pitch in at your end.

The hunting season was very satisfying. We bagged forty-four snow geese in two days, which isn't bad for this city boy. I also visited some processing plants in Cleveland situated right on Lake Erie, which may be of interest to us down the road.

Good luck with Black Duck. I am anxious for some dimensions on those promising veins. Please give my best to your lovely wife.

Best regards,
Walter

St. Lawrence Corporation Ltd.
St. Lawrence, Newfoundland
October 22, 1933

Dear Mr. Siebert:

I hope this letter finds you and Mrs. Siebert well.

I have made arrangements with Mr. Aubrey Farrell and Mr. Gregory Giovannini to advance credit to the men so we can start work on the property. These gentlemen run the two general stores in town and I have had to promise payment from us by Christmas in order to shore up the agreement.

I am not sure any of us can appreciate the hardships in this neck of the woods, so it is a good sign of cooperation that Mr. Farrell and Mr. Giovannini would agree to advance us the funds. I hope you agree.

Timing is also critical at the moment as we have a small window between the Newfoundland inshore fishery and the winter Grand Bank fishery. Men will soon commit themselves to a bank schooner and will be gone from the community for up to four months in the early winter. We have to pay the men now if we have any chance to get some strong backs on our side. This part of the coast doesn't usually see snow until December, so this next month of work will be critical for us.

Unless I hear otherwise, then, I will hire fifteen men, pay their back wages, and proceed to do reconnaissance work on the Black Duck vein.

As you can see, I'm using the first sheet of letterhead you sent up. I'm glad the incorporation is finally in place. I realize we have a lot going on right now, but I don't want us to lose track of our shareholding agreement. It was a major decision for me to accept a lower salary now in exchange for equity in the corporation, but I feel I should be invested in this future as I help build it.

Best regards,
Donald

St. Lawrence Corporation Ltd.
Room 1116, 120 Broadway
New York 5, NY

October 29, 1933

Dear Don,

I note with some irony the date as I write you. How anyone could think they have suffered more than those of us clustered around the New York Stock Exchange on this date four years ago is frankly testimony to how well we Americans have weathered this depression with our usual fortitude. No wallowing in it, I say, and we all make our own futures.

So I was somewhat dismayed to read the terms you have agreed to with Mr. Farrell. These men should be thankful for any work in that desolate corner of the world. However, I appreciate your local knowledge, so quickly absorbed. Let's hope I can raise the capital in the short time you have given me. Please keep me apprised of the work so I can throw around some dimensions when I do the tour in the city.

I will caution you, Don, to be aware that those charming Irish people are very good at putting one over on us straight shooting American types. Be careful about stories of starving and barefoot children. I could tell you some stories from Mexico where your esteemed boss was taken for a naïve fool, so I have learned a thing or two.

Best regards to your lovely wife,
Walter

St. Lawrence, Newfoundland

November 1, 1933

Dear Dorothy,

How are you my darling sister? I am hoping that Ivah and Mother and Daddy have been keeping you up-to-date on our little adventure. We are settling into our boarding house where I sometimes feel we are too well looked after since I had imagined my married life would begin with slaving over a hot stove and tending to my beloved, much like you and Bill. I hope you know I am teasing, dear one, and it is closer to the truth that I admire you and Bill more and more as I begin my married life.

I knew things would be different for Don and me given the adventure we were undertaking. But the truth is I am not seeing much that resembles the picture I had in my head. Of course that picture was probably at odds with living in a small room in a small house in a small town in a small country. To be honest, that part isn't as hard as I might have imagined. The hard part is watching Don start a mine from a small room in a small house in a small town in a small country. And with what seems to be a small amount of money.

Don't tell anyone at home, but I don't think anything at the mine site is as Don was expecting. He doesn't say much about it, but his sleep is always troubled. He is consumed with getting this right and I can see he steps very carefully as his every move is watched and interpreted. I encourage him to talk to me about it when we are alone, much as I saw you and Bill in your early days. But my heart could burst when I look at him and I see so many ways to bring happiness into our married life. I cannot imagine a day without him.

Please find time to send some news and give Bill a big hug from his favorite Crammond. The post here works much better than I had anticipated. At least something is not as I pictured.

Big hugs to you both,
Urla

St. Lawrence, Newfoundland

November 5, 1933

Dear Pop,

I have just an hour to get this letter off to you before the mail comes or else it would have to wait a week or two. The weather is closing in and it's occasionally too stormy or foggy for the mail boat to make it into the harbor.

Your last letter made good time and it's always great to hear the news from home. I'm not sure anyone would be surprised to learn that Paul DeNilo went down in a mob shooting. Even as kids we knew something wasn't right in that house. But you needn't worry about the Italian mafia here. There is only one family group, all descended from a few brothers who came to Newfoundland from Italy in the 1860s. They left war behind in Europe and came here to engage in the salt fish trade. They send salt fish to New England and bring back goods for their general store. The family is from the north, and have pale skin and blue eyes, bearing no resemblance to the more suspicious crowd from the south of Italy. So I don't have to watch my back here.

In fact, on several evenings now I have visited Mr. Gregory Giovannini, cousin to our landlord of the same name. By the way, that happens a lot here, so it is a town of nicknames. Our landlord goes by Dudler, not Gregory because there are too many of them. There is a Rubber Jack Fitzpatrick to distinguish him from the other Jack Fitzpatricks and on it goes. Urla wonders why in a town of 900 people there couldn't be more variety in their names!

I enjoy Mr. Giovannini's company very much and he is full of stories of the early days of the salt fish trade. He is a darn fine gin rummy player too. Like so many around here, Mr. Giovannini almost lost his business when world trade collapsed in 1929. There is a general store left but the business is only a shell of its earlier glory days. It still amazes me to see how far-reaching are the effects of the '29 crash.

The government here has yet to recover. It is faced with empty coffers, high unemployment, and desperate people in every outport and town. I don't tell Urla this, but it is far more impoverished than I was expecting. Of course the government now does everything it can to raise money even if it's self-defeating. You cannot imagine the tariff situation in this little country. Everything you hate about government is on display in spades. All goods that come through Newfoundland customs have a flat 65% tacked on before they add the duty so you can imagine how expensive things are. As a result, many people living in this part of the country smuggle from the French islands of Saint Pierre and Miquelon. It took this Methodist boy a while to get used to it but things are so much cheaper there, even compared to the U.S., that I now accept it as the only way to do business around here. Sugar, for example, is ten cents a pound here, but two and a half cents a pound if you bring it in from Saint Pierre.

Of course "bringing it in" can get a little hair raising! The vast majority of people get things through unnoticed, but there have been some dramatic confrontations at sea with the Coast Guard, and the stories get more embellished as they pass from house to house—and funnier! Last week they caught a fellow trying to smuggle in a piano.

For now, I am happy to get American cigarettes through a neighbor for $3.50 a thousand. I hope to go to Saint Pierre before Christmas to pick up the machinery that Siebert is shipping and hopefully a bottle or two of cheer.

You'd be happy to know I managed to get a couple of hours of hunting last week. It was quite an affair as everyone here loads their own shells, so I will have to learn how. They are using old muzzle loaders traded here for furs by the Hudson Bay Trading Company. You have probably never seen this many ptarmigan, or what the locals call partridge, in your life. The hills here are full of them. I was after ducks though and shot four nice ones. It was a terrible day of weather and if it had been the least bit calm I would've had enough to last all winter.

I'm not sure what we can do about Christmas presents. The only way to avoid duty is to send items that are over a year old and critical to the household. All the bathroom fittings we brought with us are useless to us here as there is no pipe. I've asked Siebert to send that in, so I'll test the tariff rule on that shipment. Otherwise I may arrange an address in Saint Pierre so you can send things.

I would very much like you to include in the package from Siebert my old sewing machine motor, complete with wiring and the pulley that fits against the wheel. The machines here have no foot action and have to be cranked by hand. I have never seen such poorly made clothes and the men all need better waders and coats for the mine. Urla is anxious to make some clothes too.

This week "Doc" Smith arrived back in St. Lawrence. He is a geologist and has been here since Siebert started working the lease last year. When we arrived in St. Lawrence, he was in Germany visiting his wife and eight children. I guess he is the de facto manager of the operation although this has never been made clear by Siebert. Thankfully, he and I get along quite well and he is leaving the engineering and surveying sides clearly to me. At any rate, it will take two of us to make things work, so I'm happy for his company. He is staying at the same boarding house, and both Urla and I enjoy stories of his experiences from Russia to South America.

Best regards to all and I will write again when the next boat comes in.

As ever,
Donald

Water Street
St. Lawrence, Newfoundland
November 15, 1933

Dear Mother and Dad,

I must laugh as I write the address at the top of the page. I felt it was time to have proper stationary and proper salutations. Everyone in the house looked at me strangely when I asked what street we are on. First of all, the streets are barely roads, and secondly, everybody is so well known how could the mail go astray! So I felt like a silly city girl, and not for the first time.

Yesterday I had a caller to see me at the boarding house. Mrs. G says there are always a few nosy ones who have to meet the new people in town! So I sat politely and had tea with a Mrs. Annie Pike. She is my age, but looks fifty and has never been outside the town of St. Lawrence in her life. The big thing she wanted me to know about her is the fact that when her sister died they sent her to Halifax to be embalmed. I nearly gagged on my tea but acted suitably impressed at this fact. I never know what the afternoon will bring.

You will be pleased to know I've become a dedicated churchgoer, although maybe not in the way you envision. Every evening I have been accompanying our landlady, Mrs. Giovannini, to church to light a candle and say a prayer for a few men from the community. Along the way, we call upon a few others and eventually the children of one of the men, a Mr. Louis Etchegary.

There is so little opportunity here that some of the men have taken work smuggling liquor by boat from the French islands close to here into New York. In fact, the tots of Glenlivet you both have in the evening could well be thanks to these men! They have been doing this during much of the Prohibition and have been careful to not find themselves inside U.S. territory. However, on this last trip they weren't quite so lucky. Apparently, their ship, called the Which One, strayed inside the limit while making a handover. The Coast Guard arrested the whole lot of them and they are now sitting in jail in the Bronx. It appears that the fight to end the Prohibition is not going out without some fireworks!

The Etchegary children lost their mother a few years ago, so you can imagine there are lots of prayers joined with theirs when we go to church in the evening.

I have been adding to my language glossary too. This week Mrs. G asked me to "Sing out to Walter. I'm after running out of flour." That meant I was to tell Walter to go to the store for his mother. Their language is peppered with the prettiest kinds of words.

I will write again very soon. Don always reminds me we have to catch the mail boat before it leaves or else you'll be worried. But please don't worry about us. Although the place is rough, the people have been very sweet.

Love to you both,
Urla

St. Lawrence, Newfoundland

November 18, 1933

Dear Mother and Daddy,

Wind has delayed the mail boat, so I thought I would send you another quick note today. It might keep the mail boat down, but not the women of this town. Mrs. G declared this morning "It's a grand day for a line of clothes." The whole town has clothes drying, and flying, horizontally on long lines and the town looks like it is celebrating something.

I laughed at Daddy's comment that I must be growing gills from eating so much fish up here. While this is primarily a fishing village, the fishing has been so poor and the prices so low that not many are fishing right now. But everyone has a flock of sheep, pigs, and cows, so we have plenty of lamb, pork, and beef. Some days we have duck or ptarmigan. And everything is eaten with potatoes. Don says many of the men who work with him go through a sack of potatoes a week.

Our real treat is cream of wheat in the morning, but only if it has been smuggled in from Saint Pierre. If you have to buy it in the shops here it is sixty-five cents a package. Oranges are three for twenty-five cents, so you can imagine how few of them are eaten.

On the other hand, you can get a pair of wool socks for sixty cents. Everyone here wears all homemade and homespun woollens. They shear their own sheep, spin their own wool, and knit up a storm. I'm surely the only woman in this country who doesn't know how to knit but I'm intent on rectifying that soon.

Don is working so hard at the mine and I am so proud of him. Since he arrived they have built a two truck garage, a workshop, a house for the crusher and one for a compressor. I'm not sure what all of this is, but he seemed pleased!

They are very short of medicines here and I'm wondering if you could send some things for them to keep out at the mine site? I told Don I would ask you. They need two large bottles of iodine, two large bottles of Argyrol, and six medicine droppers. It will be wonderful if you could send those out and Don will reimburse you later.

I hope you're not working too hard, Daddy, and that you have enough time to give Sturdy his daily walks. He must be feeling a little lost with both Ivah and me away at once.

Love to you both,
Urla

St. Lawrence, Newfoundland

November 20, 1933

Dear Mom, Pop, Howard, Edith, and King,

Well hello from your daughter-in-law. I'm sorry it has taken me this long to check in from our new home, but we have finally settled in and I thought it would be a good time to write.

We really couldn't ask for nicer people to stay with. Their house is among the nicest in the town. Many of the houses are very rudimentary, some of them elevated on posts with no cellars and no attics, and it always strikes me as odd that the place with the worst weather has the poorest house construction. The wood around here doesn't lend itself to strong beams and grand houses. It is short scrub pine and spruce, and hardly any use for firewood even. Most of the houses are heated with small chunks of wood and also coal that comes in from Nova Scotia, Canada. There's usually only one stove and that's where everyone gathers as the weather turns cold. On the first cold evening, Don and I turned back the bedspread only to find beach rocks, hot from the stove, inviting us in to a toasty bed. What a treat!

I would love to take a photograph to give you a better idea of our surroundings, but instead I will test my descriptive abilities to make you feel as though you are here.

The hills all run down to the sea to make this lovely protected harbor. At the head of the harbor, the rocks run straight up for hundreds of feet forming Cape Chapeau Rouge. On the other side is a matching granite formation, slightly smaller, called Calapoose. There are no marshes or dunes or flats. In fact there are no easy transitions from one piece of geography to the next. The sea meets an abrupt end everywhere it touches whether it's a cliff face, a rocky beach, or a big patch of alders. In many ways, it's like so much around here: all hard edges, hard lives, and hard stories. I will admit it is overwhelming to me at times and I long for the softness of my life at home.

On the other hand, I'm starting to see glimpses beneath the hard exteriors that are intriguing. When I expected that soft, idyllic image of a remote village, I now realize the people would have been soft too. The hardness is an adjustment, but I'm starting to see that the trade off in terms of people may well be worth it.

Don is terribly busy at the mine and working seven days a week. He is determined to get fluorspar on the wharf as soon as possible. I am glad he now has the company of Doc Smith, who entertains us at night with stories and is a great bridge player too.

Mom, you would be thrilled to learn he is an ideal husband. Just as you counseled, I left his socks exactly where he dropped them for two days and he got the message and has been more attentive ever since—well-considered advice!

I must also write Ivah today and want to get both these letters on the Glencoe, hopefully tomorrow. Sometimes gusty winds will keep the mail boat from entering the harbor, so I will pray hard that these get to you tomorrow.

I hope this finds you all well and excited for your Thanksgiving feast. We will sure miss the turkey and trimmings, and you all of course.

Love,
Urla

Water Street
St. Lawrence, Newfoundland

November 21, 1933

Dear Ivah,

I hope you notice my official address now that I am a chatelaine on Water Street. Thanks for the news from Bucknell and your booklist. I love hearing about your classes and all the work there is to do. Don't be too taken in by your roommate, as I'm sure she has moments of feeling very doubtful herself, even if she hides it well.

I wonder could you send me some books from the list I'll attach to this letter? I had better get busy if I am to start honing my skills as a world famous writer! I have looked about in people's homes, but I've yet to see a book or a bookcase and I'm a little afraid to embarrass them or me by asking. To be honest, I was expecting perhaps some literary provincialism but I wasn't expecting a literary wasteland. Oh dear. Luckily I have the cold to take my mind off the isolation.

There is a library in the town of Grand Bank, where we stopped on our way to St. Lawrence. But I'm not yet desperate enough to venture onto another boat, so I am taking my time reading the books I brought with me. Anything you can send me, dear Sis, would be well appreciated.

I am slowly coming to know some of the women in the town. There are two sisters, Ena and Gertie Farrell, who have come calling a few times. I am seesawing between young women my age who are unmarried but barrels of fun, and married women who have so much to teach me that I would like to sit at their feet all day. But they are already carrying the weight of children and housework so the last thing they need is a puppy like me around. They never seem to complain, certainly not in my presence, and carry about their days completing enormously under-appreciated tasks. And there is little respite from the housework. I think of Mother painting dishes in the afternoon or sitting quietly to read or needlepoint. That seems a world away.

But the other day I thought of something: maybe it is incredibly important that these women use their intelligence simply to manage the household, and to make life as normal as possible for everyone around them. It is a very noble role. I have never really seen it that way.

Then there are times when I think of how awful my days would be to not have options or to imagine what else I might do in my life. Don has mentioned that mining is opening up in Mexico, and on days when I feel impossibly cold and damp I imagine me under the bougainvillea trying to cool off.

I wonder if the women here have dreams like mine? I don't know anyone well enough yet to ask, but from what I see, their options are so very limited. Yet no one looks miserable, and at the risk of oversimplifying, I am now starting to see this perhaps as a bit of a gift in that they know what the future holds for them. I'm trying not to panic at the fact that I don't have a clue about what it holds for me.

Let me get this finished so I can make the mail boat. I hope there will be some more news from you when the Glencoe arrives.

Love to you both,
Urla

. . . .

Since the letter is still open I will tell you about a recent cultural highlight! Everyone was excited that a new movie was coming to town. You can imagine our reaction when we heard it was Charlie Chaplin in City Lights so that tells you something about how far behind we are. They also had the Passion Play showing. As it was strictly a Catholic affair, Don and I decided to go on Saturday as the Passion Play was on Friday only. But the priest here is very wise and knew that the Friday night audience didn't need the Passion Play, so he saved it for the wicked devils on Saturday night. We were seated right up front and couldn't leave without being noticed! Bet you haven't had a Saturday night like that!

St. Lawrence, Newfoundland

November 22, 1933

Dear Pop,

Thanks for your last letter and I accept your criticism that I'm writing more about the place than the work. I know it must strike you as funny that we could find so much to talk about in a little town of 900 people. It surprises us too!

So onto the work.

I finally managed to get the men paid for some back work and now have a great team working on the Black Duck site. While I was waiting for the financing to come through I ran a few survey lines into the mine, through some of the toughest country I've ever walked through. I certainly won't need to worry about gaining weight! This site is further advanced than I was expecting from Siebert's account. By that I mean the size of the exposed vein and the quality of the fluorspar. The mine site itself, on the other hand, is just a ramshackle operation and not quite as Siebert had described. He has firmly told me there will not be enough money to pay the men and improve the facilities, so I am sticking to just being able to pay the men. I am hoping to sink a new shaft this week. Mostly though it's an open pit.

The plan is to have 2,000 tons of fluorspar on the wharf by this spring. We will ship it to Dominion Steel and Coal Company (DOSCO) in Sydney, Nova Scotia. If it meets their standards then we have a going concern. The ore in Black Duck is very high grade with up to 95% calcium fluoride and very few contaminants.

Right now it's more like a deep sewer trench than a mine. The water problem is acute. I can see that going any deeper at the Black Duck will be difficult. The motors that Siebert sent with me are helping for now but we have had to repair the main one twice already to stay ahead of the flow. I have ordered good pumps and pipe to come to Saint Pierre, where the lack of tariff makes them affordable.

I am heading over there in a couple of days and will have more to report then. I will check out the market for wrought-iron products as you asked.

For any packages you want to send, address them to me in care of M. A. Maufroy, Saint Pierre and Miquelon. That should do it. We are heading over principally for dynamite and hope to pick up a ton to bring back. The boat is also taking over about twenty empty boxes that will come back labelled 40% dynamite, but will carry everything from truck springs to false teeth.

I would like to get a good supply of gas from Saint Pierre but that doesn't look possible. All our gas here comes from the Imperial Oil Company of Canada who has a ten year monopoly. I swear they're shipping all their junk here because we get at least three gallons of water in fifty gallons of gas. We have a problem keeping the gas lines from freezing tight so that adds to our woes.

I took a trip up the coast the other day in an open boat to see the original discovery stake that was placed there years ago. From the water you could see the wide vein of fluorspar glistening in the sun and I could see why it attracted attention. I've never seen so many ducks in my life and then just ahead of our boat were "jumpers"—porpoises to you. All in all it was one spectacular day on the water.

Good luck with the squirrels in the attic. Here there are no attics and no squirrels, so we have left behind some problems at least.

As ever,
Donald

St. Lawrence, Newfoundland

November 22, 1933

Dear Dorothy,

Mother and Daddy have passed along your news and I am so thrilled for you and Bill. I know you have always wanted a house full of children so hats off to you for getting started! I am sure Bill is excited to get another little Scotsman into the Mutch clan. Daddy, too, of course, and I'm sure he's secretly praying for a boy to offset his life of girls.

It is impossible not to think of children in a town like this. I have never seen so many youngsters in all my life. Right in our own boarding house there are four adorable ones that keep us all busy and entertained. Don and I both have lots of fun with them. Blanche is the youngest at three and I've never seen a healthier child given what's available to eat here. Walter is six and a real boy who waits for Don to come home every day to be thrown around like a football. Leonis (yes that's a girl's name) is quite bashful, but I hope to do some sewing with her if we can ever get Siebert to send us a machine. Alfred, at eleven, is quite an artist and a very likable boy. Completing the picture is Mrs. G, who is very progressive and intelligent. Mr. G is the most industrious man, for his small size, I have ever seen.

This is also the smallest family in the community! I have learned that small families generally mean that children have died in childbirth or at a young age. Certainly there are small crosses, lots of them, in the cemetery. The town still bustles with children in every yard, on every path, and in every meadow.

They are at once beautiful and pitiful. Some of them surely exist on bread, fish, and potatoes and take turns to eat. But I will say a washcloth is licked over every one of them in the mornings on the way to school because it's hard to find a child looking Dickensian, despite the poverty. I see Mrs. G dropping off some of her homemade blueberry jam or loaves of bread to some families and I wonder how any of them are surviving on so little. It has been a terrible time in this part of the world. Oh I know it has been everywhere, but this really seems exceptional. No one complains, certainly not to me, a stranger, but it is very simple to see now that I have opened my eyes.

I guess I didn't allow anything to disturb my vision of an idyllic village life. How infantile of me. I am somewhat ashamed of my short sightedness. The sheer number of mouths to feed would shock you and, given the hold of the Catholic Church on the community, I don't see the numbers dropping.

Mrs. G's neighbor told me she had eleven children in eleven years. I was sure she had to be wrong about that and I spent a good part of last night working out my mathematics. One child a year is not at all unusual.

So over to you, my darling Dorothy. Bring this beautiful healthy child of yours into the world and give them every opportunity, as I know you and Bill will. Our love to you both and let me know every ache, pain, and the joyful bits too.

Love,
Urla

St. Lawrence, Newfoundland

November 30, 1933

Dear Ivah,

I was thinking about you today as I know you are writing your first exams and submitting those dastardly final papers. I can sure appreciate how stressful yet enervating this time is for you. I think I was homesick for all that excitement because I was feeling very moody and blue this morning. But Mrs. G has convinced me the fog does that to everyone.

You may think you have seen fog. Even Don, who crossed the Atlantic twice, thought he knew fog. But here we are dealing with something in a category all its own.

The fog is relentless. I have come to believe I will be permanently blinded when my eyes have to adjust to sunshine. I think we are into our fifth straight day of not being able to see across the harbor. In fact, you can barely see the house next door or your own feet. I don't know how people can find their own home when the fog rolls in. I've heard reports of it being foggy for weeks at a time and I think I would go mad.

The only good thing about the fog is that it softens the hard edges of the town. All around the harbor, the cliffs disappear sharply into the sea and every rolling hill is interrupted with knobs of granite. If you were painting this scenery you would only need fine brushes. The trees are set in the oddest angles thanks to the wind (when it's not foggy it's windy). Even the people are chiselled somehow. There's not a soft line anywhere. So perhaps I'll be grateful for the fog for now for providing some relief from the hard lines.

Then I have days where I wonder why we would expect nature to be soft anyway. Maybe this landscape is the more natural one and we have softened everything around us unnecessarily. Don thinks I'm trying to trick my brain into not missing the soft rolling hills of New Jersey, but I'm not convinced. Anyway, let's just say there are days the hardness doesn't bother me so much.

I even managed to find a "reader" from Mr. Aubrey Farrell next door and discovered a wonderful Newfoundland poet to share with you.

"Erosion"

It took the sea a thousand years,
A thousand years to trace
The granite features of this cliff,
In crag and scarp and base.

It took the sea an hour one night,
An hour of storm to place
The sculpture of these granite seams
Upon a woman's face.

E.J. PRATT

So my dear sister, here are my musings on this soft foggy day. Say a little prayer that tomorrow will indeed hurt my eyes and maybe even bring a hint of winter and Christmas with it.

Hope your days and mind are not foggy at all. Good luck with your exams, and report in whenever you have a chance.

Lots of love,
Urla

Bucknell University
Lewisburg, Pennsylvania

December 12, 1933

Dear Urla,

I'm having a lonely spell tonight and sad that you are so far away.

I miss you as a confidante and have had to make due with Meryl Lawson who is the only other person here from Nutley. She will do in a pinch. Do you remember her sister Charlotte played French horn in the symphony? They are all quite serious but dependable.

Vanessa runs hot and cold and I seem to be mostly encountering the cold. I am so impressed at the men who flock around her like chickens (okay like roosters) and I have to admit that I like being part of her entourage.

Last night Vanessa referred to my nose (always a sore spot as you know) as "assertive." What in God's name does that mean? Remember Daddy used to kid me that my nose came in the room before I did? Anyway, no one has enlightened me about alternate parentage so I can only assume it was a miscalculation on God's part. I'm hoping when my sister becomes a world famous author she can pay for me to get this nose looking more patrician.

I would love to cut my hair into a nice bob but I think the curls would spring to attention and never lay neat like everyone else's. I need your advice badly.

Thanks for your poem and you're right—there's a lot of sharp edges but your Mr. Pratt softens them beautifully.

At my end, we just finished an entire semester of Carl Sandburg. I'm sure you'll remember how he describes the fog arriving "on little cat feet" and how it looks over the harbor "on silent haunches /and then moves on."

So try giving that fog of yours some feline features and that might help you get through the bad days. Speaking of which, our exams go very late this year, so I won't be heading home until the 23rd of December. By then I suspect I will be blue and moody having to have Christmas without you.

Lots of love,
Ivah

St. Lawrence, Newfoundland

December 17, 1933

Dear Mom and Pop,

I'm not sure how many more letters will get to you before Christmas. I imagine you are all getting ready for the season while here they have yet to have a snowfall and most days are gray and rainy. Not a hint of Christmas in sight.

We really have no idea how it will be celebrated here, but I don't imagine it will be a lavish affair. Just a couple of weeks ago, Urla and I attended the mass to pray for those who died in the earthquake here several years ago. We normally don't go to these things, but we were so shocked to find out there had been an earthquake in this part of the world and to imagine people had suffered from that as well as everything else that has occurred in the last couple of years.

On November 18th, 1929, there was a massive earthquake off the Grand Bank of Newfoundland, resulting in a tidal wave that struck this peninsula. Twenty-seven people died and the whole peninsula was devastated. The earthquake and tidal wave struck without warning, affecting over forty towns and villages and about 10,000 people. St. Lawrence was hardest hit in terms of loss of property but no one died. A committee addressed all the claims, and people were compensated to some degree but, coupled with the world recession, this has left the area more fragile than most.

Compounding the loss, many around here say that the fishery has not been the same since the waves hit this coast and its fish banks. As a result, the men lost much of the one method of making a living that was left to them, inshore fishing. Add to that the desperate financial shape of the Government of Newfoundland, and you have a population very dependent on the dole and scraps of work here and there. It's been a help to me of course in looking for men to work, although the need to be paid by Siebert is that much more critical. I would say a third of the families in St. Lawrence receive government assistance.

I'm heading over this week to the French islands of Saint Pierre and Miquelon. They are only sixteen miles away by boat and I'm hoping Siebert sent some of the piping I need. I hope you managed to get the sewing machine included in the shipment. It still seems strange to me to have to go to another country to get the equipment and materials we need for this mining venture but the tariff here is one heck of a pill to swallow. I know the government is desperate but talk about cutting off your nose.

I'm hoping to get some perfume and cigars to send your way for Christmas, so keep your eyes on the mailbox.

Lots of love,
Donald

Bucknell University
Lewisburg, Pennsylvania

December 19, 1933

Dear Urla,

We have had our first light snowfall, so I'm getting excited about the end of term and getting home for Christmas. Only one more paper due and home I go.

I am bursting with news on the romantic front. On Saturday past, the Phi Psis invited three sororities for their Christmas dance. I had four dances with William Gibson, which left me light headed and giddy like a schoolgirl. William is an old friend of Vanessa's and I knew he was interested a few times when he came round to collect her for class. I'm going to enlist her help before we break for Christmas and see if we can't make something happen. I would love to invite them both to the city to see the new Broadway musical *As Thousands Cheer*. Apparently Irving Berlin works his magic and you know I love Leslie Adams so I'm dying to go. I will keep you posted, dear Sis.

We will miss you so much around the house and I don't really want to speak of it so I shall not. Just know that we will be thinking of you and missing you very much.

Lots of love,
Ivah

ADELE POYNTER

St. Lawrence, Newfoundland

December 23, 1933

Dear Mother and Dad, Ivah and Sturdy,

I can hardly believe the date as I write it. I thought I would have lots of time to write given that very little was happening in the lead up to Christmas. Then one morning, the whole town sprang into action and we haven't stopped since. It must be common practice to paint at least your kitchen for Christmas, so everything is taken out like we would for spring cleaning, the room painted and reassembled. Then we started in on some serious gift preparation. Every evening, Mrs. G's friends would come by with the sleeve of a sweater or one sock left to go and knit furiously trying to keep their craft secret from the children. I hesitate to bring out my petit point, which looks so tiny and silly among their practical work. I may just attempt knitting to get me through the winter although I dare not trouble anyone to teach me now.

The Christmas baking has been a lesson in fortitude and flexibility. The basic flour here is what they call brown flour and is all you can get during the depression. Trouble is it tends to go rancid and it's not unusual to find weevils in it. One solution is to add copious amounts of molasses and a handful of raisins to make the most delicious cookies. But the resourceful women of this town have also been putting aside treasured amounts of white flour, so yesterday we made all kinds of treats, including shortbreads, pinwheels, and cinnamon buns for Christmas morning.

Don made the cinnamon buns possible by bringing back cinnamon, nutmeg, and ginger from Saint Pierre. He was brimming with excitement over all the fine things that can be bought there and how welcoming the French people were. He also brought home a hangover that looked to be about the size of a bottle of rum! He promises there will be more treats on Christmas morning.

. . . .

Don and I just came back from an evening walk. There is still no snow to brighten the darkness. Part of me is really starting to like this little town. But everything takes on a new malevolence in the dark. Walking home with no lights anywhere I wonder where in God's name have we found ourselves?

Of course you can't stay introspective for long in this little town. Just as your mind wanders and you are miles away, it's quite possible to run into a cow or a chicken, which brings you back to reality quickly. I think I told you there are no real roads in town, just paths that wind from house to house. They're always filled with animals, and the cows in particular will accompany you right into your house unless you chase them. The animals here run wild all year and sometimes wander miles away. You don't see them until the cold weather sets in and they return home to the right places. The oxen then get hitched up to homemade sleds to haul in the wood when the snow gets deep. Everything here feels part of a big story to me.

We will miss you this Christmas but I am working hard not to let that ruin my first Christmas with Don. We will find all the happiness we can and hope we don't get beach rocks in our stockings.

Love,
Urla

P.S. Give big hugs to Sturdy for me.

P.P.S. I forgot to tell you how the whole town's prayers came true. Remember I told you about the men put in jail for smuggling during the Prohibition? Well, the Which One *arrived in the harbor a couple of days ago to great fanfare! The men had spent twelve days in jail before a well-known mobster named Vannie Higgins managed to get them free. That will tell you who is benefiting from the Prohibition!! Probably just as well that is now over. Mr. Louis had a joyful reunion with his children and brought back with him a barrel of apples and a radio, the second one in town. The first one belongs to the Catholic priest!*

24 Wayne Pl.
Nutley, New Jersey

December 23, 1933

Dear Donald and Urla,

We received your Christmas letter yesterday although there was no card attached, so I don't know if that will come later or got lost in your local post office. I hope you two can get through Christmas without too many lonely moments.

We have our turkey and all the trimmings set for dinner here with Howard and Edith, Aunt Meta, Uncle George, and Kenneth. I am sure we will see the Crammonds at church on Christmas morning. Then, on the 27th, we will all head into Radio City for the Rockette show.

I hope your trip to the French islands was successful and we look forward to the perfume and cigars. That may be a perfect way to send the furs you promised when you left. I hear there are plenty of beaver and mink pelts about the place. Don't trouble yourself though, my darling.

We sent your card early and took your advice on not sending presents. We don't want the government to take any more of our money with those crazy tariff charges.

Love to you both,
Mom

1934

St. Lawrence, Newfoundland

January 7, 1934

Happy New Year, Mother and Dad,

I can hardly believe we are into 1934 as we finish up the twelve days of Christmas in our little town. We were hardly expecting this kind of celebration in a place that is struggling so much. But a celebration it has been.

On Christmas Eve, we joined Mr. and Mrs. Giovannini and the children at mass at the Catholic Church. Everyone walked, greeting others as we went around the harbor. Drawn by the lights of the church, eventually we could hear vespers being sung. The entire town attended this service as the priest went by boat the next morning to tend to other communities. The mass was sung in Latin (Don said it was all Greek to him) and the whole experience was highly ceremonial.

At home that night we put up the tree after the children went to bed and woke in the morning to their squeals and the beautiful smell of balsam fir. Don surprised me with a box of French candy and produced a bottle of champagne just before dinner. I have no idea how Mrs. G managed such a grand dinner for all of us, but we ate like kings with two large chickens, salty navel beef, roast potatoes, pickled beets and cabbage. It was all topped off with a sherry trifle. How wonderful to share that day with this special family. I gave Don one sock that I had managed to knit surreptitiously, and he laughed sweetly but reminded me he is a biped!

Starting that evening, there was something on every night up until January 6, the feast of the Epiphany. Christmas here is a twelve day affair with every day offering another round of music, story telling, singing, dancing and going from house to house where every night the food and drink seem to multiply.

Don had been very excited to get the new pumps installed at the mine just before Christmas and soon realized that would be the extent of the work from the men until today. It was wonderful to watch him have a break too and he became a very popular dance partner in the evenings!

The story telling left me fully enraptured. At times I would just stand and stare while this inexhaustible flow of words came pouring out from someone's mouth, regaling the room with some incident from the other side of the harbor or down the road or anywhere that really isn't very far at all but gets the attention of some global event. The audience gives back to the storyteller everything he needs to be encouraged.

It's like there is no other way or no other means for keeping everybody together in that room at that time so the flow of words continues and no one wants to miss out or make a sign of leaving.

There's much more to tell of course but I will get this on the next boat. I'm looking forward to hearing the news from home so hopefully our letters will cross over the Atlantic.

Lots of love,
Urla

Bucknell University
Lewisburg, Pennsylvania

January 8, 1934

Dear Urla,

I can hardly believe I am back at school already. Christmas went by so quickly and of course it wasn't the same without you at home. Granny Crammond and Dot and Bill came for Christmas dinner, which was uneventful as always. We saw the Poynters at church but Mrs. Poynter never makes an effort to look our way. Maybe our Scottish heritage really seems to bother her. Mother is not amused!

My excitement was going to Broadway with Vanessa and William. Moss Hart and Irving Berlin have a masterpiece on their hands! The theater was full to capacity and it's a great sign that the Depression is finally behind us. Ethel Waters and Marilyn Miller were terrific, but to be honest, I was so excited sitting next to William that it could have been a high-school band on stage. I am crazy about him, Sis, and I just hope he feels the same. I told Vanessa and I'm hoping she will grease the wheels of our romance.

Classes are back with a thud and we are now taking Arts Appreciation, hardly my forte.

Lots of love to you and my favorite brother-in-law,
Ivah

ADELE POYNTER

St. Lawrence Corporation Ltd.
Room 1116, 120 Broadway
New York 5, NY

January 6, 1934

Dear Donald,

I hope this finds you well. I had hoped to have better news on the financing front although I have yet to give up hope. I'm making progress with the Wayne Bank, otherwise there are very few interested in supporting an independent mine. Almost to a man, they advise me to sell the licenses to a large mining venture and secure financing that way.

As a result, you will have to approach your merchant fellows and ask for an extension with the wages until I have better news. I will leave it up to you what you tell them exactly, but my guess is we will have to encourage them to advance credit to the men until we can sell the fluorspar in the spring. This is not ideal, but I know you are the man to keep everyone moving in this direction.

I think you will also agree it would be wise to delay building you a new house until we get some of our ducks in a row.

I want you to know I haven't forgotten our agreement on your shares in St. Lawrence Corporation. My suggestion would be to formalize things when I'm ready to declare dividends.

Otherwise, I hope you and your beautiful wife are coping well. Mrs. Siebert and I enjoyed a wonderful Christmas season and spent a few days with friends on their estate in the Hudson Valley. The weather was mild, but I hear now some snow has accumulated.

Best,
Walter

St. Lawrence, Newfoundland

January 7, 1934

Dear Mom and Pop,

Happy New Year to you all. We received your Christmas card just as we were recovering from our own twelve day celebration. We both loved the Courier and Ives painting on the cover, which made us both nostalgic.

I surprised Urla with some fancy French food that I picked up in Saint Pierre. It was the perfect addition to our Christmas day dinner. Mrs. G produced her own loaves and fishes story with a table worthy of a king. Urla surprised me with a sock knitted by her own hand—a new skill courtesy of our next-door neighbor. I'm hoping the second one comes before the winter is over.

You would be very proud of your son's popularity during the dances. I have never danced so many squares, and these people can go as long into the night as the rum lasts. But the most entertaining for both of us is what they call mummering. Without warning, there is a knock on the back door and in they come, a group of five or eight, dressed in all kinds of regalia, faces blackened or shielded from the host. They sing, dance, and play music all the while we have to guess who they are. This went on every night of Christmas, and you could hardly believe there are enough people in this town to fool you but fooled we were. Then all hands have a drink and something to eat and off they go to another house to try their luck. Apparently, it's an old English custom started on Boxing Day, which is known as St. Stephen's day here.

Still waiting on word of financing from Siebert. We are so close now to getting ore on the wharf that I don't want to lose momentum.

We are going through what everyone here says is the worst winter in years. We already have about three feet of snow on the level and up to ten feet in the drifts. Snow doesn't fall here but comes in absolutely horizontal on the high winds. The sun is very low in the sky. Every morning someone will announce if we have had "frost," which is another way of saying freezing weather. Ten degrees of frost is ten below zero.

Dorothy and Bill sent us a subscription to Colliers as a Christmas present and three of them arrived in yesterday's post. They have finally directed my Popular Science magazines to this address so we have plenty to read at the moment. I suppose by now you have had notice about the Saturday Evening Post. I hope you folks like them and can share them with Howard and Edith.

I joined Father Thorne last evening for a good chat and his favorite evening beverage, which happily also happens to be mine. Radio reception was excellent and we enjoyed Amos and Andy holding forth on the qualities of Madame Butterfly.

Speaking of radio: Mother, I must ask you to be careful about what you say in interviews. I know you were thinking only the people around you were listening but you must remember that almost 50,000 native Newfoundlanders live in Brooklyn today. So your comments about us being in a very primitive place are now circulating in St. Lawrence. Josephine, the daughter of Mr. Turpin, our local customs officer, has just returned from living there (on Fourth Avenue near Greenwood Cemetery). So it didn't help our cause to have your views making their way from house to house. Plus, I can't afford to be on the bad side of the customs officer.

Hope gifts arrived from Saint Pierre and the New Year is treating you all well.

As ever,
Donald

St. Lawrence, Newfoundland

January 30, 1934

Dear Ivah,

So happy to get your letter and I hope studies are going well.

I had to write you today because I know everyone wonders how I fill my days, yet I can't imagine being any busier than I am right now.

I think I told you I have met two sisters my age, Gertie and Ena Farrell. They come calling most afternoons to go for a walk if the weather allows or just to sit and chat. They are both gifted piano players and sometimes we spend an hour playing and singing. They are very worldly given their isolation here and I continue to be amazed by this. I am hoping once Don is finished with the new sewing machine that we can use it to rework some clothes into the latest fashions.

Last night, Mrs. Giovannini and I went calling to the neighbors and found there was a party at the house and what a party it was! The house looked dark from the outside, and inside there were about thirty young people—all good dancers. We danced square dances for hours then ate partridge soup, homemade bread and butter, three kinds of delicious cake and tea. Around one in the morning, we started playing games, and at three a.m. we were having the last square dance!

Don and Mr. G knew the time we got home and I'm sure we will never hear the end of our short visit at the neighbor's.

As much as I love being here with the Giovanninis, I am looking forward to getting our own house. I want to establish some good patterns early in our married life and to take care of my own nest. Siebert had promised to build us one, but now this snow is firmly on the ground and I don't see that happening.

By the way, snow that falls here stays until the end of spring. It doesn't get pushed or removed and everyone accepts the isolation, as they do the cold. I sometimes wonder if the lack of questioning and simple acceptance doesn't lead everyone to greater happiness.

Hope you are finding lots of happiness these days and I look forward to new reports on this William character.

Lots of love from your very busy sister,
U

St. Lawrence, Newfoundland

February 15, 1934

Dear Mother and Daddy,

I haven't heard much news from either of you, so I hope that means you are okay but the post office is simply shut down! Here we don't have to worry about that because it's simply a matter of bringing your mail to the coastal boat. In fact it is in the harbor at the moment, so I hope you don't mind that I will be quick with my requests.

First, I have learned to turn the heel on a sock, so I am ready to go to greater production. Would you mind sending me some 4-ply wool in navy or gray so I can continue with my newfound passion? Don finds the local wool to be a little too scratchy for his tender American feet!

Second, I have taken on a small group of girls in a reading circle and I'm in desperate need for some books to pass around. I have five bright young women who were forced to leave school early to take care of their siblings, in some cases due to the death of their mother. I can't imagine their double tragedy. Two of them, Florence and Kathleen Etchegary, told me their father simply said, "Today will be your last day at school so pack up your desk and bring it home in your book bag." No more warnings than this. They told me they walked home around the harbor with their heavy book bag hitting their legs, and with every step they cried.

They are so keen to learn and I love their company. Don comes along and plays cribbage with their father while I gather the girls to read aloud, discuss and dream about wherever the book takes us. I'm wondering about anything by F. Scott Fitzgerald? But really anything you can find (perhaps ask at the church?) would be appreciated at this end.

Our mail is already causing great wonder at the post office so that will really add to our sense of mystery. Miss Fewer, the postmistress, can always tell me who wrote to us before we even get the letters! She studies the post-mark and return address and the handwriting with great ambition. She's a grand old lady who has been very good to us.

Don has gone over to Little St. Lawrence today to survey. He has a wonderful day for it—as the air is warm and the sun bright. On days like this, the combination of beautiful sky, snow covered hills, and deep blue water makes me wish that I could paint. Today the harbor is almost covered with ice, but it has broken into big pieces around the shore and boats can enter alright. This area doesn't usually see icebergs, but apparently a few years ago a huge one floated past the entrance to the harbor and caused some anxious moments.

I took small Blanche for a walk yesterday with our usual supply of lollipops to aid our mountain climbing. Before long we had an invitation to ride on a "slide." The passengers sit on a crossboard, rest their feet on the runners, the driver shouts, and away the horse runs with us holding on and squealing with delight. I had forgotten how much fun winter can be.

I hear there were two engagements over Christmas! Betty and Sam are going to be married in February, and John and Edna sometime in early June. It must be catching.

Lovingly,
Urla

St. Lawrence Corporation Ltd.
St. Lawrence, Newfoundland

February 20, 1934

Dear Mom and Pop,

I can hardly see out the windows as I write. We have a hard southeast wind and snow blowing in every direction, shutting down the town. Of course that means no work today at the mine, so I am enjoying a very rare day off.

I have such a good crew with me that we have been working Sundays and around the clock. Even with this weather, we are hoping to have the final shipment of ore on the dock by mid-March. That should make Siebert happy and finally bring some money into this operation.

I am in a real bind waiting for Siebert to deliver on the men's wages. I am assuming the lack of news from you means my account has not been topped up either. He has already written that our house, the putative house, is looking unlikely this year. I haven't told Urla yet.

At least he delivered on the pumps and piping, so things are going very well on the work front. In early April I'll be going into St. John's for a meeting of all mining interests in Newfoundland. There are a couple of big companies, American Smelting and Refining Company is in the center of the island mining copper and zinc; and there's a big iron ore operation near St. John's. Of course, these are all major companies and no one will be there in the bush league like us.

Thanks for including that sewing machine as we have cobbled together oilcloth into decent coveralls for the men. Urla is after me to buy yards of French lace when I am next in Saint Pierre so she and her friends can adorn their clothes. I am as surprised as she is to find a strong sense of fashion in this isolated spot. We've met many people who project a cultured air despite having nothing. Urla likes to say that around here a sense of dignity is baked right into the bread.

Thanks for the news, Pop, on the Vincent Methodist church. I cannot believe it will be celebrating one hundred years. However, I don't see me contributing to the cause until Siebert pays me.

Thanks for sending a Christmas box to Saint Pierre. Just when we will be able to get there depends on the weather and believe me we are in the throes of a real winter. Yesterday the mercury in our thermometer went into the bulb and has yet to come back! My only casualty was a pair of frozen ears and I was surprised to find out how warm snow feels when you place it on the frozen parts.

This weather has been really playing havoc at the mine. Water is still our biggest problem and you get a lot of freeze and thaw here. In the middle of a big cold snap last week, the wind shifted to SSE and along came the rain. The water started to run like a river and then three hours later it froze. You can now skate from here to the mine.

We have had some swell fish to eat, fresh frozen herring. They are caught about thirty miles from us in Fortune Bay. Apparently, they caught an octopus in the herring net the other day that took the world's record for size. I hope we don't have that on our plate tomorrow night! Of course there are families here that would welcome anything on the dinner plate. The rations here are exactly $1.80 worth of food for a month, and that includes three things: tea, flour, molasses. Getting yeast is next to impossible, so I have no idea how bread is made here every day in mind-boggling quantities. My guess is no one would be surviving here without the supplies that come in from Saint Pierre.

Now there's a place that feels very prosperous. I'm not sure how much I wrote you after my first trip there, but it felt like a different world. I knew it was French but I wasn't expecting it to be like a part of the mother country that was sliced off and placed off the coast of Newfoundland. Right from the beret on the head to the long stick of French bread under the arm, it is how I imagine any French town.

The Prohibition has been good for the French, but now of course they have to turn back to the fishery. In the meantime, there seems to be a lot of money going around. There are paved roads, shops bursting with merchandise, and good restaurants—all in a place a tenth the size of Nutley. I found people to be friendly and charming. Not many could speak English, but when the rum and whiskey started flowing, curiously so did the conversation.

Howard's gift of the Sunday Herald Tribune has been greatly appreciated. Of course the news is old, but there is such a wealth of other material that Urla and I keep it for Sunday nevertheless and share it with whomever we can. We fight over the comics first and even devour the ads. Oh, speaking of ads, here is one Urla saw in our friend Dinah's store: "Frozen herring selling here."

On that note, I will end this and hope you are all doing well.

As ever,
Donald

St. Lawrence, Newfoundland

March 10, 1934

Dear Ivah,

I have to write someone today or else go pound my pillow senseless. I finally got some truth from Don about Siebert and his promises. It was becoming too painful to watch Don's face as he became aware of having been outmaneuvered by Siebert.

First, I found out the house he promised to have built for us won't be happening until the fall and I have my doubts about that. Then, when I asked about building our own, Don admitted we have not been paid a nickel yet. Yet Don has been working so hard to keep the men motivated and there is a stockpile of ore growing on the wharf every day.

I wish I could do more to comfort him, but he does seem to be handling it well. In the small hours of the morning I can get some truth about the mine. Otherwise, he wears the party line like a mask from dusk to dawn.

Then it became even worse. Last week I was out for a walk and took a ride with the driver bringing the ore wagon back to the mine (the ore is brought from the mine site to the wharf by a big sled pulled by oxen). It was a beautiful ride until I got to the mine. I was hoping to surprise Don, but it is me who was surprised. There is very little there even just to take shelter from the weather. I at least thought there was a place for them to eat or change, and the men looked miserable and dirty. I came out as quickly as I could on the next run and didn't even tell Don I was there. I really wonder how anyone can work in conditions like that, and there is a part of me that feels ashamed.

So here is my letter of moaning to entertain you in your dorm room. On the positive side, we have been going for evening walks, unless the weather is truly forbidding. I swear the winter nights here are so crisp and clear that stars multiply right in front of your eyes. The layers and folds and intensity of all those tiny lights lift my spirits immensely.

There—I no longer need to punch my pillow. Thanks, dear Sis, for listening.

Love,
Urla

St. Lawrence, Newfoundland

March 22, 1934

Darling Daddy,

Your package arrived on today's boat and I tore it open like Christmas morning. *The Good Earth* is a perfect choice for my little group and they will be thrilled to have a copy each. I'll make sure they are well circulated after we are finished. Please tell Mother I won't write about any more adventures if she is going to become anxious and worried. Being on a slide would hardly qualify here as adventurous, let alone dangerous. Mother needs my friend Laurette's wise counsel: "Glory be to God, girl, 'tis only a bit of fun."

I'm glad you received my valentines. We had lots of fun here on Valentine's Day. The Giovannini children were preparing for it weeks ahead—Walter made thirty-six valentines. I drew some cartoons with poems for each child and dressed some lollipops in skirts and trousers. The six girls here for the card party helped dress up some pillows in Don's clothes. We put the figure in a chair, placed an antique Chinese pipe in the mouth, and waited for Don to discover his double. He got a good laugh from our antics.

Thank you for the chocolate too. I will ask Leonis to run this letter straight to the Glencoe so you can know I received your generous gift.

Love,
Urla

St. Lawrence Corporation Ltd.
St. Lawrence, Newfoundland

March 25, 1934

Dear Pop,

Mother has written to say you will be closing your New York sales office at the end of March. I know this is a blow, but I suspect a lot of small companies have pulled in their horns in this Depression. Maybe you can find something suitable near Nutley so you'll still have a place to escape Mom's chore list.

Pulling in horns is the order of the day around here. In fact, the Government of Newfoundland has just been replaced by a Commission, established by Britain, to get our financial affairs in order. Nobody seems very happy about this and it does seem rather colonial and high-handed, but the truth is a quarter of the place is on the dole. People are hungry and will do anything for a dollar.

For some people this has chiselled away at their self-respect but not everyone. I am always amazed at how many people are clinging to at least that.

Speaking of self-respect, I barely managed to hold onto mine the other day. I took a small team surveying on a beautiful clear day. We were crossing a small harbor when the wind changed, leaving us stranded about twenty feet from shore. One minute we were on solid ice and fifteen minutes later we found ourselves afloat on small ice pans. One of the men slipped off the ice and I had to fish him out with the transit tripod. In the end, it was a case of sink or swim so swim we did. It was only ten yards but a cold ten yards with all of our equipment with us. Of course, I asked if everyone could swim and all three assured me they could. They just didn't mention that they swam like cats.

We followed the telegraph poles home and I was sure pleased to get in the door. As luck would have it, there was a bottle of Saint Pierre's best in the house. The next day I woke up without even a cold in the head but a mighty fine hangover.

Both of us are feeling in perfect health and despite the cold have had no complaints or aches and pains. Urla has gained weight and I have lost it. Averaging about eight miles a day by Shank's mare back and forth to the mine has kept me very fit. Urla walks every day too, but then finds a house with fresh bread and jam and something good to talk about.

Hope this finds everybody thriving at your end too. I guess this will be all for the present and I will make a concerted effort to get off a longer letter for the next boat.

As ever,
Donald

. . . .

Dear Mother,

I will enclose a quick note for you with my message to Pop.

I am sorry you are troubled by some of the outstanding debts. Believe me, so am I. Siebert's promises are wearing pretty thin, but I am hoping that once this shipment of ore is paid for I can finally get paid. I had no idea I would be this long getting a paycheck from him. I only just found out from Doc Smith that he has not been paid by Siebert for eight months. I can't imagine his situation as he has eight children in Germany. All will be fine when the ore sells, but now with the ice in, we are hard up against it until the weather changes.

I have written everyone we owed when we left explaining our circumstances. Bambergs is the biggest and they seem okay waiting until the end of April. Everything we bought there will be put to good use when we finally get our own house. It all seems like an extravagance now—especially the bathroom fittings since there is no pipe to go with it. My biggest debt, of course, is for the transit and I have let them know it will be paid in full in due course.

Insurance and taxes at Wayne Place will have to wait, I'm afraid. I have asked Edith to send me the details on the City Opera and I am committed to helping her when I can.

This is the situation for now. Urla wants to order some seeds and we cannot even do that. So we all have to be patient and hope that Siebert comes through soon.

As ever,
Donald

St. Lawrence Corporation Ltd.
St. Lawrence, Newfoundland

March 31, 1934

Dear Mom, Pop and all the crew,

I'm writing much earlier than I expected but it's been a banner day in St. Lawrence. The steamer has made it through to pick up 1,840 tons of fluorspar for Nova Scotia. It's been one hell of an effort, but here we are. The men are proud and Doc and I are proud. We are all exhausted.

It's been fascinating to watch the piles of spar grow on the wharf. People come down just to pick it up and look at the beauty of each piece. There is every shade from pale pink and yellow, right through to bright green. We all come home from the mine so wet and dirty it seems inconceivable that we could be mining something so beautiful. I picked a particularly brilliant piece I hope to have made into a pendant for Urla.

The town turned out en masse to watch the loading operation. We laid down rails for the little cars to haul the fluorspar right into the hull. Now keep your fingers crossed that DOSCO will be happy.

That's it from my corner of the world today.

As ever,
Donald

```
TELEGRAPH
TO DA POYNTER
APRIL 3 1934
ST LAWRENCE NEWFOUNDLAND

MONEY HAS BEEN WIRED TO BANK OF NOVA SCOTIA
WATER STREET STOP DOSCO HAPPY STOP GOOD TO GO
STOP BEST WALTER FULL STOP
```

St. Lawrence, Newfoundland

April 6, 1934

Dear Mother,

What a delight to receive your package yesterday. Our mail boats have been very irregular all winter. Sometimes we get two a week and sometimes none for several weeks. We all watch the Cape to see her come around and then the telegraph office gets word that the vessel is storm bound ten miles east of here and won't be in until the morning. Waiting for the mail boat can preoccupy the whole town!

Anyway, it made it in yesterday morning and your timing was perfect. I was feeling a little lonely as Don has gone into St. John's, our first time away from each other since we arrived. It's a business trip and he left in good spirits as things are going well at the mine.

I am waiting for the Farrell sisters to visit this afternoon and watch their faces as I show them real hair curlers. All the women here use bobby pins and rags to tie up their hair at night, so you can be sure that your package will cause a sensation.

Tonight is a meeting of my reading circle. I've just loved getting to know this little group of young women. We meet at the Etchegary place, mostly because Don comes along to play cribbage with Mr. Louis, the head of the house. The family is Basque and came to Newfoundland from the south of France via Saint Pierre. Theophilus is the oldest boy. (Most of the children here are named for saints. Funny, I've yet to meet another Urla!) He has qualified as a teacher and walks eight miles in the morning to the next town and home again in the evening. The whole family is bursting with energy, intensity, and good humor.

The two girls are so lovely and I'm thrilled to be able to expose them to more language and literature. I think I told you that when their mother died they were expected to leave school and take care of their father and brothers, Louis and little Gus (named for St. Augustine). Despite that, they have maintained a love of learning and love of life that I find inspirational. When I first arrived, I was concerned no one seemed to be thinking about the future as we seem to obsess about. But I think here, not focusing on what the future may bring enhances your chance of survival and certainly your capacity for happiness.

Both Kathleen and Florence work at the telephone exchange, a pretty rudimentary one, that is located in the front room of their house. All the phone calls from the peninsula are relayed through St. Lawrence and are handled from this little room. No one here has a telephone in the home, so this is an important service. Such a contrast to Nutley, as Mr. Poynter wrote last week to say that the number of private telephones in Nutley has reached 5,000.

I'm so glad to hear that everyone is well, even Granny Crammond, who we all know will live forever. News about the daffodils and new hats for Easter was a little disheartening as we have the same gray snow that fell in December. I pine for some warm spring days and hope that will pull me from the lethargy I've been feeling of late.

For now though, the new hair curlers have perked me up.

Love,
Urla

St. Lawrence Corporation Ltd.
St. Lawrence, Newfoundland

April 12, 1934

Dear Mom and Pop,

Well let the bells ring out as your firstborn turns twenty-seven. The whole town could be celebrating for all I know as we are experiencing pea-soup fog, but Urla has been for her morning walk and didn't remark on passing a birthday parade. I appreciate the lovely card signed by all that arrived on the mail boat this week. The boat also brought a puncheon of molasses, so Mrs. G is promising the best beans ever for my birthday supper tonight.

I arrived back a few days ago from St. John's. The Depression is still very obvious in that town although it was a treat for me to find barbers and haberdashers, newspapers and a wider range of food. You would be surprised to learn that even there the clothing shops are owned by Jews and jewellery shops by Lebanese. Most of the financing and trading businesses are owned by English Protestant merchants, with the Irish bringing up the rear. There are some very impressive churches, however, which tells you a little something about priorities. Not too far from the churches you could find any number of brothels, so the town has a pioneer feel even though it is such an old city.

I walked by the seat of Government, quite an impressive building not far from my hotel. It was there two years ago that a mob stormed the building, while the Prime Minister escaped through a back door. People had enough of the poverty and joblessness. Of course the government appealed to Mother Britain to help them with their finances. The deal was struck to lend the money but also run their administrative affairs until Newfoundland proved capable of steering the ship itself. It is quite an unorthodox arrangement.

The mood in St. John's is quite unsettled as most people are not in favor of having their government usurped by the mother country. Of course, in the outports like St. Lawrence there is greater support for the new British Government Commission since they don't have a lot of confidence in the rag tag group of merchants who normally run things in St. John's. I just hope the Commission decides to give mining their support.

The best news is that money finally came through from Siebert as DOSCO paid up for the shipment of spar. I came back to St. Lawrence with bulging pockets ready to repay the local shopkeepers who have been fronting our wages. The timing couldn't be better as men are returning from the winter fishery now and will be looking for more work. I can use all the able bodies I can find as I have plans to build a proper mill. We just have to be able to high-grade the ore before shipping. With DOSCO taking everything we can produce things are sure looking up.

Please use that Power of Attorney I've signed to check on my account and let me know if Siebert has brought me up to date on salary. I would like you to pay off the Bamberg account and please send a check to Gordon Engineering for the transit.

I sure hope my account is flush since I splurged on Urla in St. John's and bought her a new blouse. She was tickled beyond belief and seems to be over a small bout of winter tiredness. I treated myself to a new pipe and some English tobacco. I've been smoking on my evening walks with Urla, but the fog is so thick she hasn't noticed yet.

I have to tell you about a beautiful schooner that put in here the other day and is still in the harbor. She is an exact picture of that *Bluenose* schooner that used to lay off the yacht basin in Englewood, only twice the size. She's here on the way to the Grand Banks for the first trip of this season, but before she goes she has to stop in Fortune Bay for a load of herring. The first few trips to the Banks are made on herring bait, the next few on capelin, which is a small fish much like a smelt (it's now time for Pop to get off his famous "three herring and one smelt" joke). After they have made their last capelin trip they come in and load up with squid and away they go. These Bankers are the most beautiful vessels I've ever seen.

I hope someday you can come and witness this yourself.

As ever,
Donald

P.S. I am enclosing the map of Newfoundland and the crosses show all of the spots where we have been on our way up here.

St. Lawrence Corporation Ltd.
St. Lawrence, Newfoundland

April 20, 1934

Dear Mom and Pop,

Well when the weather opens up here the fun begins all over again.

Last week I was smoking local tobacco and bemoaning the fact. It really isn't too bad a smoke but it takes an hour to cut and rub enough tobacco for fifteen minutes of smoke. Now here I am today smoking the finest Edgeworth tobacco, beautifully presented in a glass jar. For you foreigners, this means that we are able to get back into Saint Pierre and the goods and good times are flowing.

About Thursday, the wind hauled around to the north and took all our ice away to sea. Two nights later, in the dark of the moon, a skiff returned from Saint Pierre, bringing with it various and sundry bundles. The skipper declared the smallest bundle and then waited for an opportunity to deliver the rest to us. What a treat to get our Christmas box from you in April!

We didn't invite the customs officer to our box opening party. My slippers and Urla's collar fit exactly, so thank you for that. The skates are perfect but will have to wait until next winter. The Giovannini children bedecked themselves with beads and ribbons from the box till they looked like ancient Romans. We are saving the fruitcake until we move to our new house. I will let Urla tell you about that new development.

We have to tell you about the Christmas box from Siebert for Doc Smith that arrived at the same time. Urla is steaming mad about it, but I think it was an honest mistake. The box contained two cans of cranberries and two of blueberries. There hasn't been a day since we have arrived when we haven't had one or other of those berries on the table and lo and behold Siebert sends out two cans of each. The only thing he forgot was a can of codfish to make the job complete.

The town is looking forward to a banner year in the fishery.

Everyone is repairing their nets and traps. Skiffs and dories are all being overhauled. If there are fish out there you can bet this place will make up for the lean years when they had no fish and no price.

I am enclosing the final notes for the bank and you can tell them I will have it paid off within the month.

I'll pass this over to Urla now.

More anon,
Donald

....

Dear Mom and Pop,

I will add my thanks for the wonderful Christmas box. We think it might be better to get Christmas in April after all. The collar is very striking and I can't wait to wear it. The Christmas cake will be on offer when we have an open house at our new place. I won't delay the mail now but will write soon with a description of the house. We are both thrilled.

Spring is in the air here and there are lambs everywhere—black, white, and some so dirty you can't tell if they're black or white. The calves should be along in a month and then the town will be full of livestock. They add such a comic element it brings a smile to my face whenever I see them around.

On Easter Monday there is going to be a "breaker downer" at the hall. In other words, you dance until you drop and then you go to somebody's house for breakfast. Lent is strictly observed here, but once it is over, joy is unrestrained.

Thanks again for the wonderful gifts. Don has asked me to remind you not to send things by express, only by freight. We only need them delivered to the pier in Saint Pierre and Mr. Maufroy picks it up from there. It will get to us eventually. Parcel post is fourteen cents a pound to here from there, so don't think about sending anything that way.

Love to all,
Urla

St. Lawrence, Newfoundland

April 25, 1934

My sweet Ivah,

I was so sorry to get your news in this morning's mail. I know this William meant a lot to you. And to find out, you poor darling, that Vanessa had deceived you about her own feelings for him is a real blow.

But you must pull yourself into the strong determined woman you are and show them both you have moved on. We Crammond women don't wait for the world to come to us, so put on your best face and get back out there.

I now see that it is a luxury to let your heart rule anything. It's been fascinating for me to watch the young women here and the place that romance governs. Life is simply too hard to allow much romanticism. Yet within the practicality of their lives there's plenty of room for levity, laughter and, dare I say it, love. You will find it too.

So take heart, darling sister. There will be another William waiting for you very soon.

Love,
U

St. Lawrence, Newfoundland

May 1, 1934

Dear Mom and Pop, Edith, and Howard,

Well my May Day does not need a maypole to get me dancing. Urla has just surprised me with the news that she is expecting! We both feel like dancing although this wasn't really in the cards yet. Of course here everyone has been waiting for us to announce something since Mrs. G said the whole town knew once Urla professed to be tired.

I have also decided we will not wait for Siebert to build a house. I think I told you about old Mr. Greg Giovannini, with whom we have become quite close. We will rent a house from him that is only a few doors away from here and has a beautiful view of the harbor. We will move as soon as I make some small repairs and wire the house. Although we have all the bathroom fixtures, we don't have the piping so I have to hope that my pregnant wife won't fall off a cliff as she makes her way to an outhouse. Seriously, we are not near a cliff and we have gone all this time without an indoor toilet, so we will be fine.

Please don't tell the Crammonds if you see them at church as Urla is only writing them today too.

The *Herald Tribunes* have been coming through quite regularly and they sure are great to receive. The radio is full of static most evenings now. We don't have the radio reception we used to get because the seal fisherman are just off the coast and their radios are interrupting our service. But this will return to normal soon. In the meantime, the *Trib* is keeping me full of news although a few weeks after it happens.

As ever,
Donald

St. Lawrence, Newfoundland

May 7, 1934

Dear Mother and Daddy, Ivah, and Dorothy,

I'm thinking that you are all together on Sunday night, so I'm writing to all of you. By now you will have my letter with the baby news and now we have the further excitement of our own house.

We gave up waiting for Siebert to build us one and we are renting one only a few doors away. Its windows look right over the Cape and the view of the water could stop your heart. We are both so happy.

The house is divided through the center so that two families can live fairly privately. We have a large kitchen, storeroom, and living room on the first floor and a light, airy bedroom on the second.

Each room has been newly painted and papered. The storeroom off the kitchen has green woodwork and a cute paper of green blocks with a trim little orange flower in each block. The kitchen is painted in white with paper of white background and bright blue brush strokes. The living room has a rose-flowered paper and white woodwork. The bedroom has cream paper with small nosegays in blue, yellow, and deep pink pastel shades. I hope this is giving you a good picture!

There is a big dandy entryway off the kitchen where Don can leave his boots and hang all his heavy coats, finally getting them out of our bedroom.

There's a small open-range stove for the living room, an antique spool bed, and eight chairs that come with the house. The rest we will have to provide. Our rent is five dollars a month. See if you can beat that!

I am so excited about the garden. I have already sent to Burpee's for seeds: lettuce, tomatoes, onions, cabbage, corn, beans, peas, cosmos, marigolds, and zinnias. Don says he will dig the garden after he wires the house because he knows I would focus on the garden first.

Sorry to babble on like this, but I can't just invite you over to see so easily can I? Spring is here and I am so excited at the prospect of house keeping for ourselves.

We are having fresh salmon tonight. Some boys brought a very big one to the back door and we are indulging.

Hope your Sunday dinner will be tasty too.

Lots of love,
Urla

245 Hillside Avenue
Nutley, New Jersey

May 10, 1934

Dear Urla,

Your Mother and I have discussed arrangements for the birth with the Poynters. All are agreed that you will be coming home to have the baby. We simply cannot take the chance with the level of medical care available to you in such an isolated spot.

Old Dr. Lee is very pleased to hear your news and will be happy to take care of you. Mother and I will be happy to have you here with us too.

I hope that settles this, darling, and I'm sure Donald will be in agreement with us.

I hope this finds you in good health and full bloom.

As always,
Dad

St. Lawrence, Newfoundland

May 10, 1934

Dorothy darling,

I know you have heard my news by now and that misery loves company! Mother says you're quite tired and will be happy to get the little tyke out. I am so thrilled you will be going through this before me and able to calm all my fears and provide expert advice. I also love that we will have little ones who will know each other in a way that we missed. Here everyone has a multitude of cousins, aunts and uncles and I feel we really missed out when I watch what comfort that intimacy brings. Oh well, we are starting a new generation of Crammonds and let's hope they go forth and multiply.

I have asked Mother to send baby wool so I can turn my newfound skill into producing luxurious garments for our babies. I also requested seed packets so I can get our garden started at the new house.

I'm so excited about it, Sis—finally a place of our own where I can be the chatelaine. The house is starting to feel like our home and we never get tired of the view. You get the full sweep from Cape Chapeau Rouge to the other side of the harbor and can watch schooners come and go or simply imagine all kinds of possibilities.

I'm looking forward to your big news any day now and Don and I both send our love to you both.

Love,
Urla

> St. Lawrence Corporation Ltd.
> St. Lawrence, Newfoundland
>
> May 15, 1934

Dear Walter,

Good to receive your upbeat letter that arrived in yesterday's mail. Fred Foote had already written to say he would be coming so it was good to get clarification on his official intentions. I didn't think he is coming just to see the scenery. His brother Gordon played football with me at Bucknell so I knew that Fred had become quite a high flier in the mining sector. Sounds like there will be four to five in his entourage.

I would like to suggest you delay bringing the group until mid July so they see the mine in the best light. Right now we are shut down waiting for pumps and equipment to handle the water. We spent two weeks pumping out only to be flooded out again in one day. We have all we can do to handle the surface water here in dry times let alone when the flow increases to the size of the Third River in Nutley.

I went to the Caterpillar dealer in St. John's and they have provided me with quotes for larger pumps, compressors, and generators. This is essential if we are to support the new mill and fill orders. We are simply drawing too much electricity now to rely on the hydro power from Little St. Lawrence. I'm expecting a visit any day now to let me know that we are consuming too much of the available electricity for the town and region.

Congratulations on finding potential buyers for the mine. Let me know if you can revise your travel plans for mid July.

Best regards,
Don

St. Lawrence, Newfoundland

May 25, 1934

Dear Mom and Pop, Howard, Edith, and King,

I have to give King special mention as I thought about him so much today.

It is a beautiful spring day and I walked out to Blue Beach with some friends and then back around the harbor with them to the church to light a candle for someone sick in the community.

The town feels like a different place as the warm air teases people out of their homes and onto the front porch, into their gardens, or down to the landwash. Children are everywhere as the possibility of summer finally hits our little town. There is a place where everyone goes to play soccer, a sport that delights players and fans alike, and it has sprung alive with the warmer weather.

It would've been a perfect day to take King on his lead to prance about the place in his princely way. Trouble is he would be alone as there're almost no dogs here. Having a pet would be such an afterthought in a place where everyone is struggling. That's not to say there aren't animals. There are cows on every path, pigs along my usual walk, oxen, goats and chickens that all seem to know where they belong as it gets dark.

There's also a peculiar breed of pony, like a Shetland, that is put to good use about the place. It stands about four hands high and is a tough and strong little beast. They seem to require much less food and care so they fit in perfectly.

Our seed flats are coming along nicely although we've been warned not to plant anything outside until the risk of frost is over. We have a swell garden space and right alongside of it runs a little brook. Don and I can smell that mint growing already.

The ice is off the ponds and the kids in town are out after the trout like cats after mice. The number of trout caught is counted in dozens and it is nothing to have a young fellow come to the door and offer us twelve dozen brook trout for ten cents. They also have land locked salmon, which Don loves. The kids just land them with their poles and Don is so intrigued he has borrowed a pole from the priest and plans to go fishing next Sunday with the boys.

So please tell King I miss him terribly, and you all too of course. Don teases me that when you next see me I will be jolly fat and unrecognizable. We will see about that.

Love to you all,
Urla

St. Lawrence, Newfoundland

May 26, 1934

Dear Mom and Pop,

My first letter out in a while as we have been working hard to get another order on the wharf, this time destined for Phila. It ought to make Siebert cheerful and hopefully more benevolent. We are now getting $16 a ton, and the shipment will be over 1,000 tons.

Every letter from Siebert asks for more ore now. Since the fluorspar business is an indicator of the steel business I figured this meant the worst of the Depression is behind you. I'm sorry to hear, Pop, that is has not translated into the lamp business. I understand the decision to sell *Scout*, although it's a heart breaker for me. That's the boat that made me fall in love with sailing and I can't imagine that she won't be there for me always. But I understand that protecting the house comes first.

In mid-summer we will have a group from the States to look over Siebert's property. You might remember Fred Foote who grew up near Greenwood. He has a group interested in buying the operation and I intend to push for every nickel I can get if they want me to stay on. So I hope that no one makes an offer on *Scout* until I can afford to buy it myself.

In the meantime, have Howard go over it and clean it up so that it shines. Make sure the bilges are clean and the engine in good working order. Any speed tests should be done without the dink as she performs better that way.

Spring is here and the levels are free of snow but all the hills are still capped with ice and snow. We are having the annual easterly winds and believe me, they are winds. It has blown for two weeks from the east, bringing everything from snow, fog, rain and sunshine. When it does deal up a clear day it sure is beautiful. In the evenings we get a long soulful sunset and the whole place takes on a purple glow, bending the pink from the granite against the blue from the sea.

All the fishermen in town are getting their gear and fishnets in order and lots of them have reserved their berths on the Bankers already. You can smell tar, pitch, and oakum all over the place and after the long winter everything has sprung to life. Fences are being fixed up, nets mended, gardens dug, and wells cleaned.

The house is shaping up well and Urla is the happiest I've ever seen her. It's quite a change from being spoiled at the boarding house and quite a change from what she must have imagined. Believe me, keeping house here is not all skittles and beer. Urla makes all our own bread, and everything else that we eat. We carry our own water and wood like all the rest.

Right now the harbor is flooded with small trading schooners that come in with everything your heart could desire. We just bought half a cord of dry wood for a dollar and a half. We have to wait for the bigger boats to get vegetables but fresh meat is available any time someone butchers. We had veal the other day at fourteen cents a pound. All meat is the same price, and there is no such thing as ordering a steak or rib roast. You get the meat, and if you're lucky you get steaks and if you're not you get a chewing good time.

Of course there's plenty of fresh fish, especially flounder. They spear them with pitchforks right in front of our house and they are not a popular dish here so I have all I could want. Here the only fish is the mighty cod.

On Saturday night we went to a party and what a party it was. Nothing starts here until ten o'clock at night and winds up the same hour the next morning. This was a birthday party for a neighbor and I think they spent the last two months making cake for it. We played games and danced, and I got everyone into Simon Says and Thumbs-Up—games never heard of in this part of the world.

The party started off with French liqueurs. Then came games followed by round dances, and more games followed by square dances, then cake and coffee (real coffee too). The dances and games were eventually followed by ice cream and more cake, before all hands gathered round the piano and sang the old favorites. It all ended with "God Save the King" and we started for home. We had such a long walk that we didn't get home until 5 a.m. (the party was next door).

It was a lot of fun and we both feel that if the rest of this world would return to the simple easy times of games and dances we would all be better off. I don't think anyone here has ever heard of a nervous breakdown or kindred ills.

That's it for now I'm afraid. I have to go get more kelp for the box we keep the lobsters in. At ten cents apiece I wouldn't want any of them to die.

Love to you all,
Donald

St. Lawrence, Newfoundland

June 12, 1934

Dear Mother and Dad,

Thank you so much for the seed packets. I will start them right after I plant out our first crop of seedlings. I am committed to forcing what I can from this rocky soil. There are very few if any planted flowers around town, so the zinnias and petunias should draw crowds. Right now there isn't much of anything as it is still cool and the fog is relentless. Here it is called "capelin weather," after these small fish that roll in on the rocky beaches to spawn.

Don and I noticed groups walking past our house, headed out to Blue Beach, with buckets and containers of all kinds. I thought they were harvesting kelp for their gardens as they tend to do here but back they would come with buckets overflowing with tiny fish. If the wind was southerly you could smell them before you saw them through the fog!

Once we found out they were good for the garden, Don and I joined in the fun. At first, the site of all these fish struggling on the rocks was a little unsettling but then I discovered that females were laying their eggs in the rocks where they become fertilized by the males and die anyway. Kids are squealing and gathering them for their parents, some are even eating the eggs straight out of the females, but most bring them home to fry up and to fertilize their gardens.

Most importantly, it is a sign that the codfish will follow and summer is coming.

I'm feeling very well and full of energy. Don and I went to the dance in the church hall last night and we had a wonderful time. The hall is just above the two-room school, which is next to the church, and forms the activity and power center of town. This also includes the soccer field. Apparently, the only excuse accepted by the priest for missing mass is if you were playing soccer. Don has become quite friendly with the priest, which is highly surprising given his fondness for religion! But Father Thorne is an avid cribbage player, having learned when he was studying in Ireland. I have also discovered that Father Thorne had the first radio in St. Lawrence so Don has been catching up on Amos and Andy when I thought he was furthering his religious education.

I am happy to see him have some time off as he is working so hard on this mine. I am so proud of what he has achieved. If you could see those oxen pulling wagons of ore to the wharf you would marvel that any of this could happen. We celebrated with French brandy when the first boatload left the harbor. I haven't been very happy with Walter Siebert but I will say he has worked magic in finding customers for the fluorspar. Don has a good crew of men now and they seem to like and respect him.

Ivah has written me about your summer plans at the Jersey shore and I'm so pleased Daddy will finally close the pharmacy for a few weeks and take a break.

Can I be a terrible nag and remind you about some wool for baby clothes? Don't forget to make up a false receipt for very little so the customs officer doesn't make me pay.

That's all from our foggy end of the world.

Love,
Urla

St. Lawrence Corporation Ltd.
Room 1116, 120 Broadway
New York 5, NY

June 10, 1934

Dear Donald,

Happy to report that we are filling the orders as required and I'm working on some new contacts.

I've arranged with the Newpont boys to come in early July as you suggested. Fred has indicated that he was thrilled to keep you on there, and probably as manager since I suspect that Doc Smith will leave when I do. But of course the choice is yours to return to the U.S. as well.

I would hope to get five days of salmon fishing while I'm in that neck of the woods. Would you be able to arrange accommodation?

I'll wait to hear from you before confirming my travel arrangements.

Best regards,
Walter

St. Lawrence, Newfoundland

June 28, 1934

Dear Dorothy,

How wonderful to get your news yesterday. We are all bursting with joy at the arrival of Edward Thomas and that you and baby are doing fine. I can hardly wait to see you both. Mother says it was all without incident, but I never trust her Scottish stoicism to accurately describe anything! I hope, darling Sis, that is closer to the truth than not.

I hope your doctor visits were a little easier than mine. Last week I *joined the coastal boat in its run along the coast of this peninsula to the town of Grand Bank where there is a small hospital and a doctor. I was nervous about climbing back on a boat, my first since we arrived. Mrs. G brought me down and before I boarded I could smell cabbage coming from the stack. That almost finished me, but Mrs. G gave me a squeeze and on I went. I'm determined not to look so weak in front of these strong women.*

Don had arranged for someone to meet me and take me to the hospital and everything went well from there. The doctor says I'm healthy as a horse or maybe it was a house or a mouse. He is straight from Ireland so I am mostly taking my cue from how quickly he dismissed me. Then I was treated to pea soup, fresh bread and butter, and delivered back to the Argyle *making its way to St. Lawrence. Thank God no one was cooking cabbage on the return.*

Don was expecting a more elaborate report from the doctor, even a written one, but we have to remember having a baby around here is as ordinary as hanging out the wash. Plus the hospital is busy with so many cases of tuberculosis. This little country has a very high rate of what they call the white plague, or sometimes "consumption." There is a big campaign to inoculate young ones, but I'm not sure they have control on things yet.

Anyway, I don't want to taint this joyous occasion with any news of sickness. We are celebrating after all and Don and I could not be happier for you and Bill. We can't wait to join you in the world of babies and no sleep.

Lots of love to you, Dorothy, and to baby Edward.

Love,
Urla

Oak Beach, Long Island

June 25, 1934

Dear Donald,

Well as you can tell we have moved down to the beach. Opening it up after all winter was quite a chore and your father seems more concerned over his Jeep than helping with musty rugs and furniture. But the flag is flying high and we are at home. Most of the families have moved down by now so we've enjoyed catching up after all winter.

It's been quite hot already and I've been swimming every morning and evening to keep cool. I hope by now your dreadful fog has lifted and you are getting some warmth on your winter bones. Everyone here thinks you have gone to Greenland and I haven't bothered to correct them. It isn't that far away anyway, is it?

I'm hoping the change brings Pop out of the doldrums. He keeps going on about Roosevelt's New Deal and will it finally translate into demand for his wrought-iron products. I'm afraid ARHEPO Gifts has not had a great year. I was hoping you could help us out, darling, by paying the property taxes on the beach house this year? They are due at the end of July and we could simply take it out of your account in Nutley. Let me know if this is okay with you.

Wish you could join me for a swim this evening. I see Robert Goldman from your engineering class from time to time. He tells me he has a good job in the city supervising some new transit system. Certainly there are more jobs on offer than when you left.

I must go and find your father for a sundown drink. Please give my love to Urla.

Love,
Mother

St. Lawrence Corporation Ltd.
St. Lawrence, Newfoundland

July 12, 1934

Dear Howard,

How wonderful to get your letter on the last mail boat. Mom and Pop have kept me up to date with your job hunt. You have to remember that being a new graduate in a tough economy is a mighty challenge, so don't despair. Someone very soon will be looking for a business graduate from Rutgers with a handsome older brother. Keep a good stiff upper lip, kid, and don't let the "come back next week" boys get you.

Yes, keeping house in this burg is great, and one never has any spare time on their hands to go motoring or anything. It is a case of get up with the birds, start the fire, carry the buckets of water, take out the ashes, rebuild the fire again, as it is sure to go out while you were doing the other chores, and then maybe you eat breakfast.

Spent quite a while today and built a chicken coop. Have bought one hen and I'm going to tie it up in the coop and leave the door open. We use the hen as sort of a decoy, and try and get some more. There is a law here that all hens have to be yarded now that the gardens are sprouting. But some of my neighbors haven't heard of the law, heh heh heh.

Two rooms in the house are shared by an old lady and her sons. It is quite separate from us, but it brings me no end of entertainment. The old lady is half blind (one eye) and can't hear a thing. The boys come into her place at night and make funny noises and she thinks it's the radio. In the morning, she comes to tell us how much she enjoys the programs on our radio when of course we haven't had the radio on. She is intriguing though: she is the center of the web of communications in St. Lawrence although she never steps outside her house. They have one hen, and she has it trained to come in the back door and lay its daily egg in the lid of an old trunk.

It saves her looking for the eggs that she can't see, but her son doesn't like the idea of leaving the door open, and so they argue over it all the time.

Our neighbor on the other side of the fence is a cousin to the above one and can neither see nor hear. The trucks have more trouble with her than they do with the cows on the road. She refuses to use her own lane as it goes out past her other neighbor who she doesn't speak to, and so she insists upon using our lane. The worst of it was that her husband built a nice picket fence between our places, and every day she comes out and pulls it down, and every afternoon her husband rebuilds it, and not without quite a few misgivings, and believe me, Newfoundland misgivings are ones that invoke all the deities I ever heard of.

Around 5:00 pm every day, all of these characters forget their individual grievances and arguments and come into our kitchen to gather around the radio to hear a broadcast out of St. John's called *The Doyle Bulletin*. This is an experience not to be missed. A local purveyor of medicines and confectionary provides the radio hour. He uses the hour to advertise but also to promote songs from Newfoundland. Included in the broadcast are announcements about individuals, so people gather around just to catch up on the news of someone who has been sick or traveling or whatever. "Mr. Percy Cavanaugh of Grate's Cove would like to advise his family that his operation went well but he needs some clean pajamas." "Mrs. Effie Walsh advises her sister that the train is late leaving Lewisporte but to keep supper for her anyway."

Was out on a trading schooner to bargain with a captain who came down from Prince Edward Island with livestock. I want to buy a pig from him, but he wanted $6 and I can get them in Saint Pierre for $3. I am going to build a pen way up in the meadow, and the fellow next door is going to feed him. Please write us and suggest a name for it. I'm sure he will be a little black one, sex unknown, and if you can tell me how to tell the sexes apart please whisper it to me in your next letter.

This place is just alive at present with the migration of brown thrushes, and you can hear their twittering all over the place. We have plenty of robins, sparrows, finches, and some birds you've never seen such as bitterns and curlews. I hope you are continuing to paint the LBJs (Little Brown Jobs to this engineer). We have placed your wedding gift on our living-room wall and the two chickadees watch over us like hawks. Have you noticed how my jokes are sounding more and more like Pop?

That's it from me for now. It sure was swell to get your letter yesterday.

More anon,
Donald

St. Lawrence, Newfoundland

July 21, 1934

Dear Mom and Pop, Howard and Edith,

The mail boat has just arrived and I was disappointed to find no news from any of you. That sunshine must have you all making hay.

I did receive my latest account balance from the Bank of Nutley and I see the withdrawal for the property tax at the beach. I'm hoping Howard can soon help with some of these demands now that he is graduated as I will have some extra costs that will weigh about eight pounds and need constant feeding.

Walter Siebert left yesterday after a ten day visit. I'm not sure how serious are prospects with Fred Foote and Co. On the one hand, they are looking at five or six operations on the island, so they are serious enough. But they spent a few days with government in St. John's and I don't think they got very far with their demand for lower tariffs on mining equipment and other inputs. We will see what they bring back to Siebert.

It certainly doesn't help our cause that Roosevelt just fixed the price of gold at $35 an ounce. That's a big jump from $20 and he is trying to make gold mining more profitable in the U.S. Good for him but bad for us trying to attract a buyer for here.

Anyway, the main purpose of Siebert's trip seems to have been salmon fishing which was rather disappointing for me although I'm not sure he was much of an asset around the mine or the men. He wore fancy New England fishing attire all about the place, which makes me wonder if he had ever visited here before. We did enjoy four days on the Cape Roger river and caught some real beauties, including a fifteen pounder by Siebert. Yours truly did very well too and I brought some home for Urla, Mrs. G, Mr. Louis Michel, and of course Fr. Thorne. I'm keeping all my options open.

We had a wonderful fishing guide from a small community called Baine Harbour. I think Siebert was expecting slightly grander accommodation but he kept quiet about it. Our companion was Magistrate Hollett from Burin, a very learned man who chaired the Commission on the Compensation after the 1929 tidal wave. He had some very moving stories about loss and grief but also hard work and pure survival that left Siebert subdued for once. That color looks good on him and he should wear it more often.

That's about all from me before I head back to work this afternoon. I'm finally able to shed the heavy oiled clothing and can enjoy the walk back to the mine. The water problem continues, but we have been able to sink a fifth shaft and can now access some very wide veins of spar.

Urla continues to bloom and is coaxing what she can from the garden. We need some of your hot sunny days to make it successful.

It would be wonderful to hear from my sister on the next mail boat. I understand I could hear her on the radio in the afternoon, but that's not possible here, so she'll have to write. Even busy opera stars still have family commitments!

As ever,
Donald

St. Lawrence, Newfoundland

July 28, 1934

Dear Howard,

Congratulations on the job offer. I haven't heard the follow up but I imagine you only had to think a short time on this one. Nothing like working for your alma mater, and Rutgers is lucky to have you. Good work, kid.

While you are figuring out your salary and some other business propositions, listen to what some of the people here are facing as their business prospects.

We are in the middle of the fishing season here and you sure would gasp at the dories and the trap skiffs coming in with the cod. The price for fish is $4 a quintal. A quintal of fish is 300 weight of dried salt cod fish. Three hundred pounds of dried fish is the equivalent of 900 pounds of fresh fish, and salt costs about fifty cents for the quintal, along with all the work of drying and curing. So you can figure out for yourself just how hard a man has to work to make a living. The fishing season is actually a failure here this year, and some of these poor devils haven't landed a quintal as of yet. Just imagine facing this hard winter with less than four dollars, and no possible way to get any money.

As you might imagine, it has taken this city boy a bit of time and quite a few questions to understand how the fishery works here. It is a complex affair and I will attempt to describe it, with all kinds of allowances for my ignorance.

We have three types of fishermen here: the net, the row dory, and the motor dory. The net fisherman sets his trap, as the net is called. He visits it every day, lifts the net off the bottom and takes his fish out. He uses a motor skiff, and there are usually five to six hands in all. The whole arrangement is run on shares: the trap getting two and the men one each. After the voyage is over at the end of the season, they subtract the cost of the salt and the oil (as gas is called here) and divide the balance out into eight parts. This balance is not given to the men, but is placed at the general store to their credit for the winter. They, in turn, draw against it all winter for their supplies.

The dory man is an independent fellow, and he rows off here every morning. On the way out he stops at a little cove called Herring Cove and throws out a peculiar net. It is cone shaped, with heavy lead balls at the base of the neck, and a wood ring at the apex. This net hits the water flat and sinks to the bottom and imprisons several hundred capelin. (Capelin are a bait fish about the size of a sardine that come into the beaches to spawn.) After the dory man gets his bait he rows out about three miles and sets his trawl lines. He has these lines all coiled down in tubs in the dory, and as he rows along, he throws out the line with his hooks all baited.

They use about three or four tubs of trawl to a dory. When all the lines are out, the dory anchors for a while and the men perform that interesting Newfoundland ritual called "boiling the kettle." In the stern of every dory the men have little pails in which they start a fire and upon this they set little squat kettles, and in due time they boil the water and add the tea. After the tea is made, out comes the bread and molasses, and they proceed to "mug up."

Once this is over they start to haul back the lines. One man is in the front of the dory and the other in the stern. The front man hauls and removes the fish, while the rear fellow re-baits and passes the line out over the stern. They do this job many times, and then depart for the harbor. If the wind is fair, they hoist little "leg of mutton" sails, and blow right in the place. The fish are then landed at the stage (this is the name of the place in front of every man's home where fish is handled) and three men take their place at the dressing table. A dressing table is a queer place with funny holes and slots, but to go on with the story, all fish are handled with pitchforks just as we would handle hay, and one at a time they are placed on the table. The first man is called the throater. His particular job is to cut off the head of the fish and slit open the belly.

The second man opens the fish up and removes the gore. This is where the different holes come in. The liver goes through one, into a tub, to be made into that delicious drink made by Scott. The balance goes into another hole where it falls into a tub, which is carried up into the gardens. The fish then passes to a third man who, armed with a particularly shaped knife, splits the fish and removes half the backbone. It is the remaining half that keeps the fish together while it dries. The fish are then salted down in huge piles, and put away until it is time to dry, which I will describe in the next letter.

So there you have it, your business lesson for the day. Otherwise, our garden is coming along and peas are in blossom. Our hens are keeping up the good work since I told them an egg a day keeps the axe away.

Give my regards to Viola and my congratulations on the job.

As ever,
Donald

St. Lawrence, Newfoundland

July 25, 1934

Dear Ivah,

Thank you so much for your birthday card. It meant a lot to me that you remembered and picked one of my favorite paintings for the cover.

Today I wish I could paint since we have the most perfect summer day. My zinnias and petunias are looking a little sad, but next to us is a field of columbine, daisies, and buttercups, and when it gets closer to the sea there is a massive border of blue flag iris.

Don is at work of course. In fact, I suspect I am the only person in St. Lawrence not working today—unless you call knitting work.

Of course I do have plenty of work keeping the house going and the garden producing, but I love it. I still find some time in the afternoon to read. But for most people, summer here is far from a time of leisure because this summer fishery only lasts six to eight weeks. The men do all the catching, but the women also work from dawn to dusk.

Aside from their regular work at home, the women are responsible for curing the fish. I swear they are up long before daylight, a line of clothes hung out, the children fed, washed, and thrown out the door until nightfall, and then they make their way down to the stagehead to greet the first load of fish being brought ashore. The men have returned in their small boats from checking their cod trap. One trap could yield 10,000 to 50,000 pounds of fish, or in a bad season much less. Yields have been much smaller around here since the tidal wave a few years ago.

The fish is forked up to the stage, where the head, gut, and sound bone are removed before placing the split fish into a large tub of salt. After three to four days, the fish is "struck" and the women get to work. They wash off the excess salt and lay the fish out on flakes to dry. They have to be turned in the sun or brought inside if it rains. The dry fish is stacked inside one of the small buildings called a store or rooms. High quality salt fish is collected by large schooners and sold to Europe. The ships bring back salt in return. Lower quality salt fish is sent to the Caribbean and rum and molasses come back to help keep up the energy and spirits of all concerned!

When I think of how leisurely I spend my days, I am embarrassed. I am truly in awe of these strong, spirited women and hope some of that is rubbing off on me.

Send me some news of how my strong-spirited sister is doing. I hear Mother is not happy the Baird name did not make it into Edward's. I understand he is a feisty little chap, so maybe he has her disposition anyway.

Love to you on this picture perfect summer day,
U

St. Lawrence Corporation Ltd.
St. Lawrence, Newfoundland

July 31, 1934

Dear Mom, Pop and all Oak Beach residents,

I have a quiet evening to send you word before the week turns busy again. The price of fluorspar has just jumped a little, so Siebert wants us to fill orders while we can. I've got three full shifts now and couldn't be happier with the work ethic of these men.

I had a nice break this weekend and went to Saint Pierre with Mr. Louis and his son, Theo. With the Prohibition over, the mood isn't quite as buoyant as when I was there in December, but the place is still thriving to the visitor's eye. We had smooth sailing over, but a heavy sea and southerly wind on our return. Might I say we were quite heavy in the water on the return! Mr. Louis spent several years bringing liquor into the U.S. from Saint Pierre, so he had a number of contacts for some very good brandy and whiskey. On the way into St. Lawrence harbor we stopped and pulled some codfish from a neighbor's trap, so we had a thin veneer of fish over our ill-gotten goods to keep any suspicions at bay.

Urla doesn't miss a trick. She mentioned the perfume I brought for her birthday had a fishy smell on the bottle, but I have convinced her that her sense of smell is off with the pregnancy.

The Etchegarys bought three new violins, paid for by the church, to add to the fledgling orchestra Father Thorne is starting at the school. Theo also bought some big band music on vinyl records, so the dance prospects are looking up.

Thanks for the news of the beach. I guess it's a good sign if there are three new houses being built. Has Howard been fishing off the pier? Is anyone getting King in the water?

I am very tempted to get a good gun dog here. They raise terrific setters on the next peninsula and I might check them out in the coming months. I've had many offers to go partridge hunting as soon as the weather cools. I'm confident my gun will do the trick, but a good dog would guarantee success.

Back to the salt—I mean fluorspar mine tomorrow. I understand from Siebert that Fred Foote and Co. did not make an offer after all. I suspect Siebert was asking too much, but the government here has cut off its nose to spite its face. It will not give any investor a tariff break on machinery.

Beautiful sunny day here although the evenings are cool. No tall drinks and canapés on the deck for us!

Love,
Donald

St. Lawrence, Newfoundland

August 15, 1934

Dear Mother and Dad,

Thank you for the lovely skeins of wool which arrived in yesterday's mail. Mrs. Mary Turpin has shown me how to knit the most divine matinee jackets for babies, and I have already started one in blue for Edward. I still have lots of time to finish one for my own sprog, who is growing more evident every day. I still have four more months to go and around here women don't put their feet up until the midwife walks into the room.

I had the most delightful surprise today. Do you remember me telling you that I have a group of young women and we read books together? Well this morning they came calling with a picnic all prepared, a woolen blanket, and copies of our Hemingway novel. (After Don went salmon fishing with the Magistrate Hollett and told him about our reading circle, he arranged to have books sent over from a small library in Grand Bank. So very thoughtful of him.)

Off we went on a lovely walk to Haypook Pond, where we had the most wonderful picnic full of laughs and stories and fun. I have never laughed like I do with these women. The youngest, Florence Etchegary, has a great sense of mischief and is full of adventure. Her long legs and wild hair usually lead the group wherever we go. Her older sister, Kathleen, is quieter but has such a generous nature that I love her company. Olivia Murray is studying to be a teacher, although she says she's not a fan of Hemingway and won't be teaching him! Priscilla Tarrant would like to make clothes for the rich and famous in New York! Lol Murray says she wants to be one of the rich and famous in New York. Some of them want to get married while others imagine themselves traveling the world and being anything they want.

We read from the book in turns and dissolve in laughter as each person attempts to sound like Hemingway. But the books have become secondary to us getting together. I get so much more from them than I give. It enthralls me that they find sheer joy and delight in language. How did I miss this when I first arrived? I think I was looking for traditional appreciation of books, as we know it. But these young women, and most people I have met here, can crack open the language of everyday living and find something extraordinary there.

So much of their everyday lives are poems onto themselves.

So it was a mighty fine day, topped off with a new knitting project. Thank you both again.

Before I close I'll give you a quick garden update. Finally the corn has tassels, and before too long hopefully ears. No one here has ever seen corn growing or corn on the cob in cans so we are a town curiosity. No one grows tomatoes either and I'm pleased to say all of ours have flowered and have promising green globes!

Love to all,
Urla

St. Lawrence Corporation Ltd.
St. Lawrence, Newfoundland

September 3, 1934

Dear Commissioner Hope Simpson:

Congratulations on your appointment as the Commissioner of Natural Resources. I have recently received a copy of the Commission's priorities for the Dominion of Newfoundland, issued on August 21 of this year.

While I appreciate you have a monumental task in formulating an economic plan for this country, I was shocked to see that mining received so little mention in your report. While agriculture is a noble area, it troubles me that your Commission has placed it as the number one priority for Newfoundland, to the exclusion of our mineral resources.

We are producing chemical grade fluorspar (CaF_2) in St. Lawrence and shipping it to Canada and the United States where it is a valued flux in the manufacturing of steel. There is talk of much greater demand in the coming years, so we are sitting on enormous potential. Our hope is to find additional markets in the United States. However, raising money in today's climate is challenging. We were hoping to count on some government intervention, particularly in the area of tariff reduction on our inputs.

Right now we are facing demands for higher wages, which will not be possible for us unless we get relief on some other aspects. The cost of diesel and other oil products to generate electricity, plus the high tariffs on machinery, means that we are a much higher-cost producer than our competition.

I understand from my colleagues that iron ore on Wabana and the lead zinc operation in Buchans are enjoying very high production too.

I am hoping you can find room in your planning to give mineral resources the attention they deserve.

Yours truly,
Donald A. Poynter
P. Eng

```
TELEGRAPH
TO DA POYNTER
SEPTEMBER 12 1934
ST LAWRENCE NEWFOUNDLAND

NEW ORDER CONFIRMED FOR CLEVELAND FOR 927 TONS
STOP GREAT LAKES CARRIER WILL MEET SHIP IN
ARVIDA QUEBEC STOP CONFIRM SHIPMENT DATE ASAP
FULL STOP REGARDS WALTER
```

St. Lawrence, Newfoundland

September 26, 1934

Dear Ivah,

I feared our streak of happiness could not last forever. Don has been working so hard and finally took three days to go partridge hunting with a couple of local men and the Irish doctor who examined me a few months ago. The trip went very well (Don says the Irish and the Newfoundlanders love to kill things!) and he came home refreshed and happy. Within hours, however, he discovered that while he was away the men working at the mine agreed to form a union. Don felt very blindsided as you can imagine.

He knew there was some discontent with working conditions, and agreed with much of what the men were asking for. Don had already requested a raise in wages but was flatly turned down by Siebert who insists there is no more money for the operation. Now they have a much bigger problem, and the union organizer, Aloysius Turpin, is a bit of a troublemaker, so watch out.

They are all meeting today, so I am hoping for some better news. I have a blueberry pie lying in wait for him, made from my own hard days work of picking. Getting down to the bushes is getting a little harder, but I still managed to join a great gaggle of girls for an afternoon of berry picking. As always, it turned into a fun affair.

Some of them can pick for hours with flour sacks tied around their waists and they pick with both hands. They will make mostly jam, but I know how Don loves a good pie.

I'm happy to hear you are settled back at Varsity. Sophomore year was very happy for me and I hope for you. Hopefully you will have a sweeter roommate than last year. It's not too early to learn that sophistication can come at a high price.

Mother has written that you are thinking about teaching as your career, and there was some concern about following so directly in my footsteps. I am honored, little Sis.

When I started at Bucknell, I really thought I would become a writer, and who knows, maybe I will still. But the whole process of teaching started to fascinate me and I could see myself helping others to love English literature like I do. You don't have to go to Uppsala College, but I loved it there and living in East Orange gave me my first real taste of being alone. Oh, I missed Don alright, but we managed most weekends at Bucknell or Uppsala, so that helped.

Since coming here I have a whole new respect for the teaching profession. I'm not sure if I told you but I bring any books I have to the convent so the Sisters can use them in their own teaching. Turns out they read them first and they have a lively discussion amongst themselves. There are days I would love to be a witness to their cloistered lives together.

I've only ever been invited into the vestibule of the Sacred Heart Convent, but it has been enough to intrigue me. There are about eight Sisters in the congregation of the Sisters of Mercy in St. Lawrence. This mission was established in 1871 by two Sisters direct from Ireland. I cannot imagine what they encountered sixty-five years ago in this place, but they stayed, built the convent, and most importantly taught school. Their first school was in a fishing shed and they taught about ninety-five students.

Eventually, one of the Sisters, Sister Mary Borgia, was bequeathed a sizable sum from a brother in Ireland, which she used to build a new church and two-room school for St. Lawrence. She is still here in the convent and loves literature, so I imagine she is a passionate teacher. They all have high standards for reading, writing, and speaking. This is obvious in the population. People may have thick accents but most speak and write very well. I have heard that Sister Mary Bernard gives them all elocution lessons, which would be a good idea even in New Jersey!

These women are true teachers in every sense and in every aspect of their lives. They invited me to come to help with reading in grades three and four. I panicked a little because I've put so much thought and anxiety into what kind of teacher I will be. After a few days watching these Sisters, I now realize I'll be exactly the kind of teacher the students need. I'm not sure it's any more complicated than that. I am in awe of their incredible sense of dedication and selflessness. I know you will be a teacher true to yourself as well.

Always good to finish a letter on the subject of selflessness!

Much love to you, dear Ivah. I look forward to an update soon.

Love,
Urla

St. Lawrence, Newfoundland
October 1, 1934

Dear Ivah,

A quick note to say thanks for the school newsletters and the Fannie Farmer cookies. I have to hide them from Don and ration them with our evening coffee.

You have probably heard that Mother and Daddy are encouraging me to travel home for the birth earlier than I would like. I know they're scared to death that I might have a baby in this primitive place. I've done a poor job of convincing them that there is some semblance of civilization here.

I am fine with coming home. But Mother's tone always has an edge—like she is worried I won't remember what fork to use with oysters! She has already made it clear to me that she thought she left knitting back in Scotland. Imagine how she'll feel about me picking berries in a flour sack!

Oh well, at least I will have you around at Christmas and that is a great comfort to me. So work hard and get home early.

My love,
U

```
TELEGRAPH
TO DA POYNTER
OCTOBER 2 1934
ST LAWRENCE NEWFOUNDLAND

LETTER TO FOLLOW RE NEW DEVELOPMENTS AT YOUR END
STOP NO ALLOWANCE PERMITTED FULL STOP WALTER
```

> St. Lawrence Corporation Ltd.
> St. Lawrence, Newfoundland
>
> September 30, 1934

Dear Walter,

Although this will take longer to reach you, I cannot risk having the contents of a telegraph broadcasted around the community. I would advise you to do the same from now on.

Although in hindsight there were a number of indications of discontent at the mine, I was very surprised to find they had gone to the extreme of forming a union. One of the men, Aloysius Turpin, has been in contact with other union members at the Buchans and Wabana mines. It didn't take him long to discover that their wages are higher, and working conditions better than here.

ADELE POYNTER

I did indicate this to you in July when you visited, as I was well aware of it from my meeting with other managers in St. John's in April. Now that we are really pushing the men to fill these new orders, Mr. Turpin has seized the opportunity to organize their demands and lead the pack.

My frank assessment is that we can appease the workers by offering a wage increase, which I endorse. The other demands, for improved conditions, can be reconsidered in the spring. This should get us through this demanding period, until financing allows us to address operational concerns here at the site.

I must emphasize that to a man, our two shifts are hard-working and productive. We are moving spar to the wharf in all kinds of conditions. I'm not sure I thought this possible this time last year.

I look forward to your response.

Regards,
Donald

> St. Lawrence Corporation Ltd.
> Room 1116, 120 Broadway
> New York 5, New York
>
> October 1, 1934

Dear Donald,

How distressing to get your correspondance about developments with the workers. I hope you received my quick reply by telegraph that I do not have the means to change any aspect of the operation right now, except to ask that all hands fill the orders I have worked hard to secure.

I have seen this nonsense before. The formation of the union is often just a scare tactic, and you will find naysayers and rabble-rousers like Mr. Turpin in every operation. It is your job to manage this and surely well within your capability.

Again I must stress there is no room for added benefits.

I understand you were away when all of this happened. I suspect you have learned that you must be on the ground at all times in a pioneer operation as we have here.

My best to Mrs. Poynter.

Regards,
Walter

St. Lawrence, Newfoundland

October 10, 1934

Dear Mother and Dad,

I thought I'd write you about an interesting visit and revelation.

Magistrate Hollett came to town yesterday and we got together with Mr. Aubrey Farrell for a fierce game of contract bridge. Don and I are becoming quite the team and our risky bidding earned us the game.

However that is not my revelation. The Magistrate brought me a book from his collection on the meaning and importance of names— a very thoughtful gift as Don and I have started to argue about baby names already. Of course I decided to look up the names you chose for us three girls. I started with Dorothy and was thrilled to find it is Greek for "God's great gift." Then I find that Ivah means the exact same thing but in Hebrew.

Imagine my surprise when I discover the genesis of Urla, a name I have never really been fond of but assumed was decreed by some Scottish Laird as meaning "Strong Lady of the Mist," or some other romantic vision. Instead I find I have been named for a town or peninsula in Turkey. In fact, Urla is a Greek word meaning marshland.

You will be relieved to know that after my initial shock I laughed and laughed. My sisters are God's great gift, everyone here is named for a saint, and I am called after a marshland.

ADELE POYNTER

I am sure someday I will get the full story from you and we can laugh all over again. In the meantime, I'll make sure my child's name is not wet and boggy.

Love as always,
Marshy Urla

St. Lawrence Corporation Ltd.
St. Lawrence, Newfoundland

October 15, 1934

Dear Mom, Pop, How and E,

I have fallen behind on correspondence lately and I hope you all forgive me. The situation at the mine is tense and deserves my full attention.

The men are making demands that Siebert says we can't meet. In the meantime, I am supposed to motivate them to increase production to fill orders. We have had a lot of rain this fall, so the pumps are barely keeping ahead of the floods. The mine is wet and cold and these oilcloth clothes simply aren't enough to keep anyone dry. We need proper rubber pants and jackets and a place for the men to change before and after shift.

I have promised (something I really can't do) that we will rectify this in the spring and that seems to have mollified everyone at the moment. I'm not enjoying doing this dance I can tell you. I have promoted one man, Celestine Giovannini, to be the foreman at the mine, and I have a lot of confidence in him. I'm hoping he can help keep production and spirits up at the same time.

The Herald Tribune has been arriving regularly, so thank you for that subscription. The coverage of parties, museum events, and shows of every description sure gives the impression that New York City has forgotten about the Depression. Days of poverty and joblessness seem very far away when you read the paper.

Urla is being a champ about my long days at the mine site. Thankfully, she has made some good friends who come calling to keep her company. She still manages some good walks around town but no more hiking to the top of Chapeau Rouge! The young women here think nothing of taking off through scrub pine and bush and walking to the top of capes, overland for good berry picking, or off to one of the many beaches for a picnic. They are as thin and trim as they are hearty. You will then find them sitting around in the evening sewing lace onto collars and remaking clothes that were brought home from someone's visit away. Perfume and hairstyles are as popular a topic here as they were in the girls' sorority at Bucknell. Not a boatload of Saint Pierre liquor is allowed in the harbor unless there is something aboard for the women of the community.

As I write this evening, Urla is practicing rug hooking, her new-found love. An English nurse has been posted to St. Lawrence for a couple of months. Her previous station was in northern Newfoundland with the Grenfell mission, where she learned rug hooking with silk stockings in the Grenfell style. When I asked Urla how her day was she sometimes kids that her biggest decision was whether to knit or hook rugs, each providing equal pleasure.

The Crammonds have written me separately requesting that Urla get home for the birth earlier than we had planned. I don't want to make any waves and have booked passage for October 30th. This means I will follow much later, closer to the baby's arrival in mid-December. I'm sure you all will look in on her and keep her company until I arrive.

I sure look forward to some good pipe tobacco. I'm down to the local stuff now and it is so hard you have to cut it and massage it, and some even chew it, to soften it enough to burn. Maybe it's a bad sign that I don't find it too bad!

More anon.

As ever,
Donald

ADELE POYNTER

The Lord Nelson
Halifax, Nova Scotia

November 1, 1934

My Dear Don,

How very strange to find myself in this hotel without you. It feels like ten years ago, not one, that we were here together about to start our new adventure.

This time around I am about thirty pounds heavier and I'm sitting in the room looking at all the beautiful baby clothes given to me the other evening. I suspect you realized I could hardly contain my tears at the kindness. The darling bonnets in every shade from my reading circle, and the matinee jackets and leggings from the Farrells and Slaneys make me so happy I can't really explain it. I now know why I could never find any baby wool! Everyone in St. Lawrence was knitting up a storm for us.

I'd rather not talk about the trip over except to say I was glad to see Halifax harbor. I had not realized you had asked everyone on board to watch out for me, so answering all their concerned questions certainly took my mind off the rocking! I met the captain for the next leg at breakfast here this morning and he says we should have smooth sailing right into Brooklyn Bridge. One part of my brain says they all say that, but I am choosing to go with the other part that says yippee.

Your little boy or girl is kicking up a storm anyway, so it will be a rough ride even if the seas are like a bathtub.

As per instructions I will have Daddy telegraph you the minute I arrive.

I hope our little house is not too lonely for you. Just close your eyes and imagine the three of us there very soon. Promise me you won't work too hard and won't practice bridge too often without me.

All my love from our honeymoon spot,
Urla

St. Lawrence, Newfoundland

November 22, 1934

Dear Urla,

I hope by now things have settled down at Hillside Avenue. It is only natural that you would've had a major adjustment in going back to your childhood home as now a grand married woman! Mother says she has been by to visit you twice and that you look well.

I ran into Ena Farrell at the post office and wasn't too happy to find out that she wrote you about Mrs. Edwards. It was a very sad affair, but you must remember that this was her fifteenth childbirth, not her first. Aunts and uncles have been recruited to take some of the smaller children and I have given her husband, Joe, time off to sort out arrangements at home. It riles me that the Catholic Church encourages this sort of unbridled childbearing, regardless of family income or health risk, but I've had this argument with Father Thorne many times and to no avail.

Anyway, you're not to think about things like this in the next while.

Celestine Giovannini has been a godsend at the mine. We are at peak production with two shifts running seven days a week. The men are happy about the extra money in the run up to Christmas, so all is quiet on the union front.

We are expecting a ship to pick up that last big order at the end of the month before weather closes in for a while. Then I'm on the next ship to New York City. Hurrah.

I see there's a meeting of Bucknell Alumni at the Harrington Hotel right after Thanksgiving. I hope you can make it and give everyone my regards.

That's it from this end for now, but I'll keep this letter open until I have to run to the post office.

Love,
Don

ADELE POYNTER

I knew I would have more news. I forgot to mention that I dug up some great carrots and parsnip from your garden of plenty on the weekend. I was worried about leaving them in the ground, but around here lots of people do. They say that they sweeten up a little giving you a wonderful surprise in May. So our baby will have fresh Newfoundland vegetables from her mom's garden next spring.

Mail boat is rounding the Cape and I am on the run.

245 Hillside Avenue
Nutley, New Jersey

November 28, 1934

Dear Don,

You will not recognize me when you see me as I have become considerably rounder. I would like to think it's all baby, but I indulged hugely at Thanksgiving. I don't remember Mother putting on such a lavish affair, but her Scottish tendencies were not in evidence on Thursday past. We dined like kings and Daddy had invited several people from the church and his pipe band. Ivah was home from Bucknell and brought three girls with her who couldn't go all the way to their homes for the holiday.

Do you think university life has changed that much since we left? I don't remember so much nattering about parties and boys, but maybe I'm just becoming an old married woman! I think they certainly saw me that way and since I wasn't aching to be part of their conversation, that suited me just fine. Mother thinks I have become very quiet at these events. I think I just prefer it when what people say actually adds up to something.

On Friday I went to your house for leftovers. Everyone was so kind. Your father seems to be spending a lot of time in Philadelphia where he says sales are firmer than in the city.

Dr. Lee gave me a good going over at my appointment yesterday. He seemed shocked that I knew my blood pressure history, and seemed genuinely well prepared for the birth. I told him I had an English nurse who had worked in a Grenfell Mission hospital and he was most impressed. He told me when he was a student he had gone to hear Dr. Grenfell speak in New York City and left enchanted.

That's all from here at the moment. I am counting the days until you both arrive, hopefully with you coming first!

I'm grateful I brought my rug hooking. Mother keeps trying to interest me in painting dishes with her, a task I never enjoyed before and certainly can't appreciate now.

I've sent some beautiful cotton fabric to the Etchegary girls. I discovered it in my hope chest and can't think of a better use. They can make shift dresses for their work at the telegraph office and I know they will love it. I've written Olivia, Gertie, Ena, and Mrs. G too, so if you see them tell them a letter is winging its way.

Daddy will mail this on his way back to the drugstore. Everyone sends their love to you, especially me.

U

St. Lawrence, Newfoundland

November 30, 1934

Urla darling,

I'm dashing you a quick note that will hopefully get to you from the Grand Bank post office. We have had three days of strong SSWesterly gales, filling the harbor with pans of ice from the Gulf. As a result, the ore ship can't get in, and nothing else either. Mr. Louis is attempting the road to Grand Bank tomorrow morning so I'm giving him this to mail.

I don't want you to panic yet, but it won't be possible for me to leave here until the ore has left the wharf. Of course, it won't be possible for me to leave here until the ship lands to take me. In any event, we need a good wind change to make either possible.

Father Thorne insists he is doing everything possible in the upstairs department to get me there.

I'll get this over to Mr. Louis now. He and I have a regular evening date to listen to *Amos and Andy*. He became a fan while he was rum running in the States and insists it was part of the reason he bought a radio. Of course half the population of the lane also comes to listen!

Keep your fingers crossed and spirits up.

My love always,
Don

TELEGRAPH
TO MR DA POYNTER
DECEMBER 11 1934
ST LAWRENCE NEWFOUNDLAND

BABY GIRL ARRIVED THIS MORNING STOP MOTHER AND
BABY DOING WELL STOP 8 POUNDS 14 OUNCES STOP
JOY ALL AROUND STOP MOTHER FULL STOP

TELEGRAPH
TO MRS DA POYNTER
DECEMBER 11 1934
NUTLEY NEW JERSEY

JOY OF SAFE ARRIVAL TRUMPS SADNESS OF MY
ABSENCE STOP WELCOME LITTLE BARBARA ADELE STOP
BE HOME SOON LOVE TO YOU BOTH DONALD FULL STOP

245 Hillside Avenue
Nutley, New Jersey

Christmas Day, 1934

Dear Don,

Not in my wildest dreams did I think I would be celebrating this Christmas without you. I think about you every moment and I'm so glad you are joining Mrs. G again for Christmas day. I can picture every part of your day and that gives me some comfort.

Nor in my wildest dreams did I think I could love a little creature as I love Barbara. She is so pink and vibrant and round that it brings a smile to my face just to clap eyes on her. She is so interested in everything going on around her that sometimes feeding can be a frustrating affair, but I quickly forgive her. She is just two weeks old today and has regained to her birth weight. Mother and Dad have fixed up my own infant cradle, so Barbara and I are quite comfortable for now.

Christmas here threatens to be very quiet and I can't help but compare to last year. Here, most of the excitement happens outside the house—in restaurants or theaters or ballrooms whereas in St. Lawrence it all comes to you or to a neighbor down the road. So enjoy it all for me please.

Ivah is home but always dashing to the latest and shiniest event, like a crow. She has been into the city a lot, taking in a number of Broadway plays. She has met some high-fliers at varsity and I wish I could like them more than I do, but I find them all quite superficial. Otherwise, it is great to see her, and she is her adorable self when she's around Barbara. Even Mother has been caught humming and smiling to herself!

Dorothy and Bill have visited with Sweet William, who looks like he will be a tall serious boy but for now is a very pleasant little chap. Bill is besotted with him and I have to admit to pangs of jealousy when I see the fun he has with him. But I'm hoping you will get to see your little girl very soon. Please let me know as soon as ship traffic resumes and we can fix dates for your arrival.

I won't last much longer tonight as I rose early this morning to a little beak looking for food, and then off to church where I bounced Barbara from one hip to the other to buy some silence. Remind me, if they ever visit, not to bring Mother and Daddy to church in St. Lawrence. Between the Latin and the multitudes under ten years old it might just be the end of them! I had forgotten how solemn the Methodists can be.

The mummers will be heading your way tomorrow night, so fill me in on who you recognize and who manages to fool you. Please give my love to the Giovanninis, big and small, and know that I think of you every moment.

Love,
Urla and Barbara

1935

St. Lawrence, Newfoundland

January 5, 1935

Dear Urla,

I know by now you have received my telegraph. I know that you are as disappointed as I am.

We certainly did not see this one coming and Celestine Giovannini was more shocked than me. We think that over Christmas, with time off and liquor really running, Aloysius Turpin was able to convince a lot of men to stage a strike. I guess we had fooled ourselves that promises made in October could keep the men going through to Spring. Now we have a real problem, certainly a bigger one, and I have to put my thinking cap on for this one.

It doesn't help that I can't reach Siebert anywhere. I know they have friends in Vermont and go there regularly over the Christmas period. I have sent telegraphs to his office and home, so am hoping for some direction very soon. I still feel showing up here in his tweed plus fours, felt fishing hat, and a fly rod straight out of the catalogue did not help convince anyone that this operation is truly strapped for cash. But that's the party line and I have to follow it and encourage the men to do the same.

On a lighter note, a shipment of goods from Saint Pierre managed to come overland through Grand Bank. The ice had dampened everyone's spirits and supply of spirits! So Christmas was made brighter with some wonderful brandy and scotch, the finest I have ever tasted. On New Year's Eve, Mr. Louis offered me delicately preserved dried fruit and chocolate and I dared not ask the provenance. Mrs. G's Christmas dinner also seemed to benefit from some foreign supplies, so there were many contented faces around the table.

For now, I will be doing what they call a "half board" at the Giovanninis. That way I can be sure of two good meals a day but go home to sleep. I've had lots of offers to help take care of me in your absence but prefer to keep things official especially as we go through this strike business.

Don't feel the need to defend me around any dinner table as I am happy to take care of that myself. I know no one there can appreciate the immediacy of this situation nor my need to be on site.

Love to you both,
Don

24 Wayne Place
Nutley, New Jersey

January 21, 1935

Dear Donald,

Urla has just left with baby Barbara so I thought I would get a note off to you this evening. She really is the most darling baby and Urla doesn't appear to have a feather out of her. I can't imagine it is easy living with her parents and I offered her a place here with us if need be.

I held afternoon tea for the Ladies Guild as I wanted them to meet the baby. I had to remind Urla to dress Barbara in the layette they had sent from Burgdorf's. She looked very handsome indeed and everyone was tickled pink. Your wife has inherited her mother's stubborn streak and for some reason always dresses Barbara in odd matinee jackets. She acquiesced today and everybody looked resplendent. We had the fine Decker china too and cream cakes, so you will be happy to know the family was well presented.

We are well into winter here. The fireplaces are going constantly and I am tired of asking your father to install central heating like the Vannellis have next door. He travels to Philadelphia a lot these days, going by train, often coming back with another salesman he has met. So keeping the house warm while he's gone is a chore. Howard seems to have eyes for no one but Violet and darned if I can figure that one out.

Poor Edith is back and forth to the city, even when it is thirty degrees outside. She is working so hard and has auditioned for some minor parts off Broadway. You would be so proud to see the time she puts in practicing.

I hate to remind you but it would be so lovely if she had a fur to keep her warm going back and forth. I understand they are very reasonable up your way and I've seen quite a few at Sunday church. Mine can certainly wait but perhaps you could find your way to send one home for E? If that isn't possible, would you mind if we took the money from your account here and looked around for a bargain?

King is scratching at the door, so I will close this letter for now.

Love always,

Mother

P.S. Pop says all kinds of opportunity is opening up in Phila and you would only be a couple of hours away.

245 Hillside Avenue
Nutley, New Jersey

February 2, 1935

Dear Don,

Well the groundhog certainly went back into his hole today, as the sun is filling the sky. I swear I could almost feel Spring when I took Barbara for her walk this morning. I think that might be the first sun she's had on her face and, like a good Poynter, she seemed to revel in it.

We left Hillside Avenue and walked along Grant, watching the squirrels scampering about in the old leaves. We stopped in to visit Daddy, aka Grandpa, at the drug store where I had my favorite vanilla soda while Barbara slept, oblivious to her many fans. That was her Nutley walk.

At night, in the quiet of our bedroom, I take her on walks in St. Lawrence. Sometimes we head down to Farrell's store, greet everyone around the wood stove, and buy molasses candy before we continue on, around the landwash, looking for bottles with messages in them.

Other times, we go down to the telephone office where Florence and Kathleen make a huge fuss over her and she plays with their balls of wool like a kitten. Maybe we go to visit Mr. Louis who bounces her on his knee, clapping her hands in time with his feet.

Tomorrow night I think I'll take her up on the high road for some fresh bread and butter at the Turpins, greeting the cows along on the way.

I'm anxious for some news from you about the strike. Mrs. G has written to say everyone is a little on edge. Keep your spirits up, darling, and hopefully Siebert will come through soon.

Although I miss our evenings around the radio, I have been enjoying the treat of having radio reception in the afternoon. I put Barbara down for her nap and turn on CBS to hear The Kate Smith Matinee. This is so wonderful and I wish we could listen together. I'm learning the words to "When the Moon Comes over the Mountain" and will serenade you when I'm home.

Yours always,
U

St. Lawrence, Newfoundland

February 3, 1935

Dear Urla,

I wish I had something to report other than Siebert's intransigence. He actually wrote that we wouldn't be working that hard this time of year anyway and can afford to delay a few orders, claiming that shipping wouldn't be possible until the Spring. He also suggested we could take on new men when they returned from the Winter fishery and then gear up production in April or May. I was impressed he knew about the Winter fishery but not by much else. He doesn't seem to understand what a strike does to motivation and trust. He also seems to forget these men support families and a strike means no money at the hardest time of the year.

I have been keeping a low profile but did go with Mrs. G to the Candlemass service at the church last night. No one here has heard of the groundhog and instead everyone carried candles to the altar to be blessed and then the church was lit only by candlelight—a very moving affair.

Of course, it's all about prayer around here now that Lent has started. After supper Mrs. G makes me a cup of coffee and I find that chair you loved to sit in, fill my pipe, and settle in. As soon as I hear "First Sorrowful Mystery: Jesus in the Garden of Gethsemane" I know it's my cue to leave. The whole family is on its knees in a circle around Mrs. G who clacks away on the prayer beads. Poor Walter always glances up at me as I tiptoe out and I'm sure he wants to escape too.

As I walk home I know that it's the same picture in every house. If a meteorite were to hit the town at this moment, archaeologists would find the whole population on their knees, with the exception of one lone Methodist on the road.

That's all for now from me. Not a very inspiring letter I know but I'm hoping something breaks soon. At least that's what I asked Mrs. G to pray for last night.

Love to you both,
Don

St. Lawrence Corporation Ltd.
St. Lawrence, Newfoundland

February 8, 1935

Dear Mom and Pop,

Thank you for your letter of January 21st. I hope the house has warmed up a little.

Things are quite tense here with the strike, but I wanted to let you know that mail is getting through. All the ice is gone from the harbor and freight is moving well. Ironically, all the lumber has arrived for the mill, a major project we will start in the Spring. I have to hand it to Siebert that he came through on that and somehow managed to get the tariffs lifted. Now if I could just get him to turn his attention to the strike. Although I don't make this position known locally, I am pushing for a ten percent wage increase, and proper change facilities at the mine site.

I appreciate your note, Pop, on negotiating with a firm hand and not letting things "turn into a circus." I can understand that, from your end, the entire situation looks like a bit of a circus. Believe me, many days I feel I am flying trapeze between the union and Siebert. But if anything goes wrong it is me who falls 200 feet to his death.

When I wrote that some of these people are my friends now I didn't mean to suggest that I am therefore blinded to the financial realities of the situation. I knew when I got myself into this that Siebert would always be scrambling for financing. But now we are well into it, the men have been working hard, we are filling orders and money is coming in somewhere. There is really no sense comparing what's going on here to the steel mills in Philadelphia. We are worlds apart.

Mother, I appreciate you reminding me of my commitment to get Edith a fur coat. I should let you know that Father Thorne was over for a game of cribbage last night and you can rest easy after I consulted him. He assures me that under no circumstances will the world come to an end if Edith doesn't get a fur coat right now.

I'm so pleased to hear that Urla and Barbara are doing well. As it looks now, she will get back here to join me faster than I will get free to join her. I will know for sure in a few weeks. Please don't say anything to her until then.

Love to all,
Donald

St. Lawrence, Newfoundland

February 14, 1935

Dear Urla,

Happy Valentine's Day to both my girls. I hope the flowers arrived this morning as requested. Mother's mood in placing the order would have depended on whether Pop kept up his end of the bargain. I hope he has learned how to buy peace at home!

On this day I am not writing about the mine at all. Instead, I will let you in on the latest goings-on in town. Remember I told you that we have had a lot of cutters coming in and out of the harbor lately, reminding anyone smuggling that they are around. Well, the other day I was coming back to Mrs. G's for lunch when Cecil Farrell stopped me on the road. He heard that a cutter was on the way from Burin with customs officials ready to give the town a thorough going over. He advised me to put away anything we had smuggled in. When I walked into the house the place was in an uproar. None of the men were home, so Mrs. G had neighbor women helping her hide things in the snow banks!

Out went cigarettes, tobacco, rubber boots, raisins, vanilla, scotch, rum and a lot more. Sure enough, about fifteen minutes later Mr. Cutter came around the Cape. They landed at the dock and hot-footed directly up to Farrell's store.

I have to admit to being a little shocked at how brutal they were. They arrive with axes and saws and can really pull a place apart and no one can stop them. They can point to anything in your house or shop and charge you with smuggling if you haven't got the original receipt.

After turning Farrell's upside down, they headed up to the Becks. Their eyes landed on the kitchen stove, which of course arrived in a full moon one night! Lo and behold they then came here. They didn't look in our old part of the house but went right through to the kitchen looking at the same stove as the Becks have, which of course arrived in the same manner. Mrs. G remained calm, and I suspect like everyone else in town was just relieved it didn't start to rain and melt the snow banks!

From there things only became more intriguing. The next day, the Magistrate arrived to try Mr. Beck and Mr. G. Of course, the Magistrate stays at the Giovannini's every time he comes. That means that for the last two years he has been eating his meals off the very stove he is here to punish them for having. He is also an old hunting buddy of Mr. Beck, so the trial should be interesting.

I will write you later with the conclusion of our little drama. Now there is a story to tell Barbara in the evening. The tide-watcher is here so I'm going to give him this letter quickly.

Love to you both,
Don

P.S. Miss Fewer is surely counting how many letters I am sending you and vice versa. I swear she gets more excited than I do when she recognizes your handwriting on the envelope. She's been very good to us and I'm hoping you bring her back a little something when you return.

St. Lawrence, Newfoundland

February 17, 1935

Dear Urla,

Well you missed a real concert at the Giovannini's at lunchtime today.

I was at the wharf receiving a shipment of dynamite, so I missed the trial. Just as I arrived home for lunch there was Mr. G arriving with two policemen in crazy fur caps and the Magistrate, who apparently is an Oxford graduate. The upshot of the trial is that Mr. G was issued a $50 fine. The maximum fine is $400 including confiscation and payment of all duty and freight that would otherwise have been charged if the stove had been legally purchased.

The two policemen sat in the front parlor while the Magistrate and I ate our lunch, cooked to perfection on the ill-gotten stove. I was waiting for Mr. G to offer us a little nip of his best French brandy after lunch but that might have been one push too far! Then they all left a little later on their way out the harbor to the next community. I am sure the whole town waved them off.

We are all waiting for you to return so we can complete our bridge foursome. I am checking into vessels this week and will book your ticket as soon as the weather settles.

By the way, don't send any more gifts without adjusting the invoice. Mr. Louis told me the girls paid a hefty tariff in order to collect the fabric you sent them. They were thrilled to get it, so please don't mention the money as I'm sure it will embarrass them.

I'm reading the *Anthony Adverse* book you left and finding it a good read.

Love,
Don

245 Hillside Avenue
Nutley, New Jersey

February 27, 1935

Dear Don,

What a treat to get your letter as I was on tenterhooks about the fate of Mr. G and the stove.

I had a get together yesterday with Nancy Dewar and Betsy Simms and we had some good laughs over our time at Uppsala. Nancy is president of the Nutley chapter of the American Association of University Women. Both of them ended up teaching in Nutley, and both left their jobs when they married. They live only a few streets from each other and attend the same clubs and activities. They seem to go into the city a lot and gushed about the latest Rodgers and Hart musical Jumbo. For my part, I gushed about the goings-on in the smuggling rings of St. Lawrence and maybe laughed too hard at my own story. I still laugh at the image of everyone storing cigarettes in the snow banks.

Sometimes I feel they all look at me wondering how I could find humor and happiness in such an impoverished environment. I'm not sure I could explain it even if I wanted to.

In the meantime, I tune out a little at all the talk of who wore what to church, whose husband is spending too much time in the city, and who was left off this or that invitation list. Quite honestly, darling, I miss the extravagance and luxury of home but not its complications.

In some ways, I think these women spend too much of their time sifting through the choices around what kind of wife they want to be. I'm so grateful I learned to be a wife in St. Lawrence where I somehow learned without complicating it. Sometimes having too many options can be a burden. I can't wait to get back where I can learn how to be a mother as effortlessly.

Speaking of extravagance, Daddy has a new line of lollipops at the drugstore, so I will be bringing home lots for Leonas and Blanche. For your birthday present, I will give you a hint: it is jazz and round.

Counting the days.

Love,
Urla

St. Lawrence, Newfoundland

March 5, 1935

Dear Urla,

I realize our letters are crossing in the mail, but I wanted to get a quick note off to you to let you know the coats arrived.

Wow, I didn't know Methodist women wore coats like this, let alone gave them away. To my untrained eye they look quite fashionable. You must have really appealed to their sense of noblesse oblige. Anyway, I dutifully brought them up to the convent. Sister Bernard answered the door and forgot herself for a moment and was all excited to receive the bundle. I think she will be delighted that the poorest women in town will now be wearing the most fashionable coats. She reminded me that families cannot buy clothes with their dole money. They were very thankful and I assured them you would soon visit with Barbara. I keep trying to get a sneak peek in behind the front door, but their life remains as mysterious as ever.

I'm sending some coins for your father in this package so let me know whether they have been lifted en route. I have some twenty, thirty and fifty centime pieces from Saint Pierre which I thought he would be interested in. They still have Napoléon on one side, which gives you some indication of their age. I am also sending the variety you can get on any day here: yesterday my pocket had American, Canadian, Newfoundland, and British coins—all in circulation here. I'm sure he would find that of interest.

Before I sign off, I must tell you I'm coming to see the radio as a mixed blessing around here. Father Thorne's housekeeper asked me the other night if I had ever had gingivitis! Naturally I was a little shocked, but I did tell her no. She then asked if I might ask you to bring some back to St. Lawrence with you. I finally got to the bottom of it when Father Thorne told me about the ad on the radio which says: thirty percent of Americans have gingivitis. This poor woman just wanted to have some too.

Much love to all the folks at Hillside, but especially you.
Don

St. Lawrence, Newfoundland

March 10, 1935

Dear Urla,

Miss Fewer tells me I must really be missing you because I am sending so many letters. It's good to know everything I do is being watched! I had to write today because the most beautiful ships are in the harbor. We missed them last year because of the ice, so I have to describe them for you.

Most large boats leave from Grand Bank, but this year a few put in here. I woke up yesterday morning and there in the harbor was a large, spectacular schooner. The sun was up and bright and I don't know if I've ever seen anything so magnificent. In full sail with her blue hull—I wish I could paint.

This banker has a thirty-man crew. She carries about twenty dories, all nestled like saucers on her deck. I was invited to have dinner with the captain. One of the mates kept us entertained with stories, and he swore they were true. He told me about drifting away from his banker when they were in the Atlantic. When they hit landfall in their open dory, they found themselves in West Africa. The stories continued in this fashion all evening.

They seem to feel the French fleet heading to the Grand Banks is very strong this year. The French government guarantees the price of cod, so that's always good for a big argument around the table.

You won't believe where I'm heading now. I saw a group of local boys yesterday with their skates, heading off to Little Pond. I stopped them and they agreed to come by and get me today. I have to put those Christmas skates to use. You would have laughed yesterday. As they headed out the hill they picked up one of the Kelly boys and I could hear Mrs. Kelly shouting, "If ye comes home drowned, I'll kill ye."

Earlier this week, I was surveying in Little St. Lawrence and was invited into the Clarke house for lunch. Without any say in the matter, I had my first taste of seal. I wouldn't call it my favorite dish. It had an oily fishy taste, much like the seabirds we have eaten around here. In other words, it tasted like second-hand herring. All the same, it was a lovely lunch and I felt quite satisfied and thrilled with the treat.

No sooner did I get home this evening and pick up the *Herald Tribune*'s recent article about Capt. Kean, the famous sealing captain, and his one-millionth seal. I don't know if you remember, but the captain of the *Portia* which carried us here is Capt. Kean's son.

In the meantime, every time I burp, I feel like there are a million seals in my belly! In this case only, I am glad you are far away.

Much love,
Don

St. Lawrence, Newfoundland

March 22, 1935

Dear Urla,

After a few nasty incidents, which I won't trouble you with, the strike is over. I suspect both Seibert and the union were fed up with the other's antics. I know I was. In the end, we settled on a five-cent raise and a new shift house at the mine. I'm not sure Aloysius Turpin and I will be exchanging Christmas cards next year.

Your passage is booked for April 6th. I have arranged all your immigration papers for when you and Barbara arrive in St. John's. This time around, you will stay on board in Halifax so you don't need to clear customs in Canada. You'll then be sailing for St. John's where you will clear customs and be met by Mrs. Ethel Giovannini who will take you to the Newfoundland Hotel for a night of luxury before you sail the next day for St. Lawrence. Be sure both of you are bundled up for the weather. Don't let signs of Spring in Nutley fool you. Yesterday we had four seasons in one day, and one of them included driving snow and biting wind.

Our little house will be ready for both of you. Lionel Turpin helped me repaint and insisted on doing Barbara's room himself. I hope she likes canary yellow!

Last night I was walking home from Father Thorne's, and all the lights were on in every house in town. My Barbara will think she is coming to live in a fairy kingdom.

The Etchegary men and I will go to Saint Pierre next weekend as we need dynamite and some other supplies for the mine. We are running low on a few other staples (I am really desperate for good tobacco) and we can't have your homecoming without champagne, that's for sure. Father Thorne kindly let me borrow the full priest regalia, just in case I need to go to the bow to bless any Coast Guard coming near. For heaven sakes, don't mention to my parents or yours that I occasionally double as a Catholic priest.

Otherwise don't expect much more news as I will be working day and night to make up for lost time. The Furness Line will send ticket details directly to you. Can I hint that a new pipe would really enhance the Saint Pierre tobacco?

Yours ever,
Don

P.S. You were sorely missed at the St. Patrick's Day dance on Saturday night. Maybe it's because it's the only relief from Lent around here, but it was a walloping good time. I ended up with the crowd at the Quirke's house having fried egg and onion sandwiches just as the sun was coming up. My legs could barely carry me home and I won't be dancing again for a while. Well, until you come home.

St. Lawrence, Newfoundland

April 11, 1935

Dear Mother and Dad,

I know you will be anxious, so I'm dashing you a quick line to say Barbara and I have safely arrived in St. Lawrence. Everyone was so kind right from when we boarded in Brooklyn to when I stepped into Don's arms a few hours ago. Perhaps it was my pale color or the distraction of this beautiful baby but we made it without a hitch. I am definitely developing better sea legs, just as long as no one cooks cabbage.

Don is smitten with his little girl. Of course he has hardly held her since we arrived. We went to Mrs. G's for lunch, and then over to visit "Uncle" Louis, Florence, and Kathleen. Barbara has been passed around and danced about in two kitchens already. Newfoundlanders adore children, although you would think they would have their fill with all the youngsters already at their feet.

Of course I caught up on the big news very quickly. The town is all aflutter over the disappearance of Father Thorne's cow. Apparently a priest simply can't live without his cream!

We are settled into our own house now and Barbara is napping in her bright yellow nursery. We will have a wonderful celebration for Don's birthday tomorrow, although I suspect it will be hard to top today. We are all very happy to finally be together. I hope that helps soften the sadness of leaving you both.

Love,
Urla and Barbara

Clifton, New Jersey

April 6, 1935

Dear Urla,

Seeing you off this morning has left me in a dreadful state, so I resolved to write you as soon as I returned home.

I sometimes wonder if you realize how happy and content Barbara is around us all in Nutley. She would grow up with doting grandparents and all kinds of opportunity, not to mention proper nutrition. I know you and Don are enjoying your little adventure in the North, but perhaps now you have to think of the next generation. From what you have described, she will be limited in so many aspects of her life and I ask you to reflect on whether this is fair.

I know you will think I'm meddling. Mother and Daddy would never say a word of course, but I don't want to continue with the family tradition of never saying how you feel. I tried to talk to you about this but found it too difficult to get past your sense of resolve.

So, dear Sis, I will leave it there. I know you saw plenty of evidence that the Depression is a thing of the past and there are job opportunities for Don all over the state.

I leave that with you and send you my love,
Dorothy

St. Lawrence, Newfoundland

April 14, 1935

Dear Mom, Pop, Howard, E and King,

Thank you all for the birthday cards and back issues of the *Nutley Sun*. Poor Miss Fewer at the post office always looks relieved when I show up as she can finally clear out her mail room. Last week I had to get a young fellow to help me carry the load home.

The best birthday present was of course the arrival of Urla and Barbara, safe and sound. Already I cannot imagine our life without this little pink bundle. Urla is resting now and one of the Giovannini girls has taken Barbara in her pram for a stroll around the harbor. It should be quite the mess when she returns as the roads are full of mud and melting snow.

It is Sunday afternoon and I'm enjoying a rare afternoon off. We are having an early Spring, so we have started construction of the new mill, something that will totally change the nature of our operation. Government inspectors graced us with their presence last week. I'm not sure if they've ever seen a mine, let alone a mine like this one. I was hoping for some help with the water problem, but they were mostly concerned with shafts and ventilation. With them was a young geologist, hired by the new Commission Government. He's a real firecracker, and a graduate of Princeton. He will be a great help with the grading set-up at the mill, but even better, he has taught me to play chess, and now Urla is keen to learn.

Sorry to hear business is slow, Pop. I keep getting mixed signals about whether the Depression is behind us or not. Siebert says demand for steel is growing and Urla says Broadway has recovered to full houses. Here fish prices are still very low, and I see demand for coal is too. Gold prices are not rebounding either. Perhaps Roosevelt's New Deal will start yielding dividends soon. Certainly, Pop, we could use your lamps here.

You would have laughed at what Urla brought back to St. Lawrence. I got plenty of pipe tobacco, so I shouldn't complain, but there is a lot of wool and sewing supplies to go with it. Then I thought she had lost her mind altogether when I saw so many silk stockings: odd ones, discolored ones, holey ones. It turns out she has great plans for hooked rugs. The women here dye the stockings using lichen, mosses, and berries. Then they cut them into little strips, hook them through burlap, and turn out some mighty fine results. Urla is planning to hook the old Crammond house in Edinburgh as a gift for her parents' 30th wedding anniversary. Mums the word.

The days are getting longer now and it's a good feeling. It's been a long winter and the strike made it even longer. Siebert has been quiet, but I suspect he will spring to life soon and announce new orders.

As requested, I paid the property tax on Wayne Place and Oak Beach for you folks.

Again thank you for the birthday wishes. I'm able to walk the barrens here in fine fashion which is not too bad for an old feller.

Love to all,
Donald

St. Lawrence, Newfoundland

April 30, 1935

Dear Dorothy,

I wasn't quite sure what to do with your letter, but I now think it was very fine of you to write me your thoughts and concerns. I would hate it if you didn't feel comfortable enough to be frank with me. I'm only sorry you didn't feel you could talk to me while I was there. The truth is I loved many parts of being home, especially being near you all, but also the comfort and availability of life's little indulgences.

Maybe I was so focused on my new baby that I didn't register much outside of that. Darling sister, please know that we have capacity for all kinds of happiness, coming from all kinds of experiences. I can only imagine that from your distance my life here doesn't look like much. But my life feels happy enough as I am living it. For now, that is the only thing I can commit to.

You will be pleased to know my cultural life has taken a big swing upwards. On Don's last trip to Saint Pierre, he bought a new radio! He has really missed having a dependable one, although it gave him a great excuse to visit Mr. Louis or the local priest in the evenings, the source of the only other radios in town.

Because we are on the south coast of this country, we receive excellent radio reception, apparently stronger than St. John's. We get WOR Gabriel Heatter just like we were sitting in New Jersey. Lowell Thomas and Boake Carter are keeping us up-to-date on the news. Yesterday evening we enjoyed Harry James and wished we could be dancing somewhere. We also get Canadian radio stations, with CJCB from Sydney, Nova Scotia, especially strong. It's not popular with everyone: Florence Etchegary told me her little brother Gus gets up early to turn on Wilf Carter, filling their little house with cowboy songs before he leaves for school. They're thinking of hiding the radio in the mornings!

Barbara gets outdoors most days except when the weather is particularly foul. Right now that is one day out of three. But if it's any way possible, somebody comes to the door after school and offers to take her for a walk. Maybe these young girls are happy to get away from chores at their own homes, but they seem to love "carting," as they say, Barbara all over town. They bring her back just before dark or if she's hungry. I've never seen anything like it.

One day Don was walking home from the mine and came upon Mary Kelly pushing a pram. She walked along with him, talking up a storm. He was surprised when she came as far as our house, and even more surprised when he discovered that his own child was in the pram. I laughed so hard I had to take a seat to recover. Mary told me she told him it was Barbara, but he said he hardly understood a word she said from the beginning of the walk to the end.

There will be a dance at the church hall this Saturday night and Don and I are going. Gertie Farrell will look after Barbara. She is marrying Theo Etchegary soon and says she wants some practice.

I better wrap this up before bedtime.

Love from your hard-to-understand sister,
Urla

St. Lawrence Corporation of Newfoundland Ltd.
Room 1116, 120 Broadway
New York 5, New York

May 4, 1935

Dear Donald,

I received your telegraph this morning about the accident. A shame indeed. Please extend my sympathies to the man's widow.

I trust by the time you receive this letter you will have filled out an accident report for government with a copy sent to me. Please have the shaft repaired as soon as possible so we don't lose too much time coming into our busy season. I have already contacted the Dawe lumber company in St. John's, so you should have heard from them by now.

Your question on compensation is a good one. I must admit I never really thought this through, and I'm surprised it was never a union issue. Regardless, it behoves us to do what's right for the poor man's family even though we don't have a formal obligation. I would offer his widow half a year's salary. That should help keep everyone fed until she can make other arrangements.

Best regards,
Walter

St. Lawrence Corporation Ltd.
St. Lawrence, Newfoundland

May 15, 1935

Dear Mom and Pop,

I know the mail has been slow from this end, but we've been through one hell of a time at the mine.

We have had mixed snow and rain for the past four weeks, so the mine has been like the trenches of France. We installed two new pumps, but it's coming in faster than we can pump it out. It looks like all that water rotted out the base of our first shaft. Two weeks ago, just at the end of the evening shift, the support beam snapped and fell on Bobby Clarke, one of the men I hired when I first arrived. I was on site that evening and glad of it, but the poor fellow was already dead when they brought him to the surface. I was quite staggered by it all, but of course had to keep my head. He worked alongside his brother and cousins and friends, so you can imagine everyone was shook up. I realize now that I had never seen a dead person before, let alone literally on my watch.

Someone ran for the priest who arrived in the town's only truck and gave the poor fellow his final rites there and then. Then we placed the body in the truck and drove to the Clarke house. By the time we got there, news of the accident had been well ahead of us. I was almost glad of the crowd that had gathered out front because I would not have enjoyed the pain of facing that poor woman alone. As it was, Father Thorne accompanied me, which helped the situation enormously.

I guess I always knew of the danger involved in this operation. But now that danger has the face of someone I knew and liked, and that changes everything.

Poor Urla. It sure hasn't been a bed of roses since she returned. We were just recovering from the ugliness of the strike, and now this. I'm afraid I haven't been great company. She is a real champ though and now with Barbara as her sidekick she is busy calling in on friends and still has her reading circle and sewing group.

Barbara is six months now and occasionally tells me she misses her Grammy and Grandpa. I tell her that maybe someday they will jump on a big ship and come to visit.

Until then, love from us all here,
Donald

St. Lawrence, Newfoundland

May 20, 1935

Dear Ivah,

Thinking about you this morning, my dear sister. I'm trying to convince Don that Barbara's first word was 'sis' but he is not buying it! As I write, she's outside the door in her pram in the sunshine, the first real warmth we've had since I arrived. I'm so excited today that I dug out the seeds I brought back with me, determined to get better results than last year.

Last week we even had snow flurries. This didn't bother anyone here and as they all say "May snow is good for sore eyes." Talk about finding the silver lining!

I took Barbara yesterday to visit her Newfoundland "aunt" and "uncle," and she's starting to get quite a few. There was a big discussion, well more of a friendly fight, over who has the best garden in town. I bet you didn't know gardening was a competitive sport! Uncle Rennie Slaney has appointed himself my new gardening adviser, so I will report soon on his magic. Now if I can just get the last snow out of the garden!

Just as Don was recovering from the mine strike and then the awful accident, now he's got himself up against the Catholic Church. It turns out that Mrs. Clarke, the widow of the man killed, took half the compensation given to her just last week by the company, and turned it over to Father Thorne so that mass can be said in her husband's name for eternity or some such thing.

Don was furious and flew across the harbor to see the priest. Father Thorne was steadfast that the money given is a sign of the woman's faith and would provide her with as much or more comfort than the money itself. They had a major blow up over this (or so the priest's house keeper has told half the town). Don came home shaking his head and mumbling about whether the church will be feeding Mrs. Clarke's seven children.

For Don this is hard to square with his view of Father Thorne as a reasonable and intelligent friend. But the pull of the church in this community would be difficult to comprehend unless you witnessed it firsthand. The church is the center of the community and involved in education, music, entertainment, commerce (they own the cod liver oil factory), and of course, soccer. The first priest came to St. Lawrence around 1850. Faith runs really deep here and I almost envy them for it. Going to church and praying at home trumps everything, except soccer, but only because that is also held sacred by the church.

On the other hand, you have never heard people take the Lord's name like they do here. When we first arrived, Don would have to whisper to me that my mouth was agape. The room would be blue with oaths, especially if someone was telling a story. Mrs. G says, "Jesus, Mary, and Joseph" fifty times a day. Sometimes it is, "Good St. Joseph," and sometimes he's, "Sweet St. Joseph." Other times, "Jesus is in the garden." My personal favorite is "Lord lifting Jesus"—which usually sounds like "Lard liftin Jaysus." Sometimes he is lifting and dying! And occasionally he is "Jumping Jesus." Poor Mother would have a heart attack on her first day here.

So, dear Sis, that's the news from here. It's so wonderful to have you to talk to. Mother tells me you are doing some student teaching this month. I can't wait to hear about it. And what about the new young man I met? Has he made any moves I should know about?

Barbara sends big bubbly kisses to her Aunt Ivah. Don and I send small uninteresting ones!

Love,
Urla

St. Lawrence, Newfoundland

May 24, 1935

Dear Mom and Pop,

"It's the twenty-fourth of May, the Queen's birthday, and if we don't get a holiday we will all run away."

That's sung by the youngsters here and everywhere in the Dominion. It is easy to forget when you are in these small towns that this is Britain's oldest colony. Of course we have King George V, not a queen at all, but apparently, the holiday still stands as a leftover from Queen Victoria. Many people in town call it Empire day.

Everyone goes trout fishing on this day with everything and anything doubling as a rod. Off they go, walking to one of a thousand ponds with their sandwiches of bread, butter, and molasses, and a glass jar full of worms. I shut the mine for the day (Siebert certainly doesn't know) since I figure no one would show up at work anyway.

Urla and I are giving a party: fresh lobsters and potato salad. Lobsters here are the sweetest I've ever tasted and they are bigger creatures than we have ever seen from Maine. They are asking ten cents each for them, so I'm not sure how many we can afford.

I know there is at least a violin and accordion coming, so it may be a long night. Urla tires quickly in the evening, but she is working hard at the garden and is busy with Barbara. Forward thinking as ever, Urla brought back several old clothes to give to the convent so they could distribute them. The word must have gone around because we had a woman knock on our door this week to say she would help Urla around the house in exchange for a coat.

I'm glad Howard and Edith are helping you open up Oak Beach for the season. I imagine everyone will take the opportunity on Memorial Day to do the same. We will be thinking of you raising the flag and eating outside. We will be doing neither, but then again you won't be having fresh lobster.

Love to all and happy Memorial Day,
Donald

St. Lawrence, Newfoundland

May 28, 1935

Dear Mother and Dad,

My garden is planted! Already I can see green shoots desperate for some warmth. Little do they know they will soon be covered in small fish and seaweed—a curious habit, but I am impressed by what people can grow here, so I'm following all their tricks. Very soon we will have rhubarb, the first fresh green that Don has seen since the last year. I imagine by now your garden is galloping, so try not to make me too jealous when you write.

We had a wonderful party in our own house the other night. It was our first one since arriving almost two years ago and we felt it was time we hosted some of the people who have been so good to us. My friends, Gertie and Ena Farrell, helped me out as they love to plan parties and prepare food. I dug out my hope chest china and they made up party favors to match. We had so many fresh lobsters and lots of potato salad, pickled beet, and jellies of all sorts.

The music was the best though. Everyone here is so musical. Someone started with "There is a Tavern in the Town," then "Put Your Arms Around Me Honey," and away the party went, carried into the night on its own legs. I didn't even realize Don had disappeared until an apparition came down the stairs. We all doubled over laughing as Don appeared, dressed as Kate Smith in a borrowed polka dot dress, supported by a couple of pillows, and a wig of wavy brown hair. He knows I just love her and he sashayed down the stairs singing "Let Me Call You Sweetheart." I laughed and cried, as did we all. From there, the fun and the songs accelerated until the final group went out the lane singing "The Last Rose of Summer." The sun was coming up as Don and I agreed our first party was a triumph.

Barbara was a champ and slept through it all. Or maybe she was singing along to her favorite songs.

Lots of love from your swinging family up North,
Urla

St. Lawrence, Newfoundland

June 10, 1935

Dear Mother, Daddy, and the whole family,

I thought I would write you all since I know you are getting together more often in the summer.

Soccer season has started with a vengeance in St. Lawrence. A team from the French island of Saint Pierre came to town two days ago and they played yesterday in a light drizzle of rain. You won't believe it, but the children were given the day off school to attend that game. As I told you, the Catholic Church takes soccer very seriously!

I took Barbara to the game and I'm glad she was too young to follow things. Let's just say neither team held back and the crowd was as vicious as the players. There were a couple of fights including *one with the referee. Many of them would make great boxers!*

Then this morning the St. Lawrence team left for Saint Pierre. I took Barbara in the pram to see them off. Well what a sight greeted us at the wharf: young men with blown-up tire inner tubes around their necks. Mr. Louis was with me sending off two of his boys to play. Imagine my shock when he told me the inner tubes served as their lifejackets! It turns out the inner tubes are very handy for the return voyage because they make great containers for St. Pierre liquor, and the customs officials are none the wiser.

I guess if they win and no one drowns on the return, it becomes a double celebration with lots of liquor to go around. Don laughed very hard when I told him what we had witnessed at the wharf, and Barbara joined him as though she understood the joke too. I think we are raising a real Newfoundlander!

The town is buzzing with the start of the summer fishery and so far catches have been good. I sure hope so as this sets up many families for the whole year. The people here deserve so much and expect so little.

Barbara is blossoming, especially now in the fresh air. She is the darling of the town, or at least it feels that way to me. Someone makes a fuss over her everywhere I go. Children are adored here. How strange that when I first arrived, I felt that most of them were neglected. They were always outdoors in any kind of weather or told to be quiet when everyone was gathered together. With so many children in each family, I now see that introducing a bit of order is the only way to survive. Mothers and fathers can seem very rough, but there is a tenderness that I somehow missed.

I hear from Dorothy that Edward is walking, so that must be fun around the house on Sundays. I sure miss seeing him grow up, but I'm glad they have you to witness it all.

Please give my love to everyone this Sunday, and to you both of course

Love,
Urla

St. Lawrence Corporation of Newfoundland Ltd.
Room 1116, 120 Broadway
New York 5, New York

June 15, 1935

Dear Don,

Good to hear from you about the progress on the mill. Properly graded ore will make a much easier sell from my end and greatly reduce our shipping costs. Do you think you can find a manager there or will I look for someone through my contacts in St. John's?

I have read through the inspection report from C. K. House. I need to know which requirements are absolutely necessary. It is not possible to do all of the upgrades and, frankly, there is no way they will force me. I am offering work to people who otherwise would be on the dole. My friends in St. John's tell me this government won't last long anyway and the whole thing is a mess. We might last longer than them.

Apparently the latest census showed a population of 280,000 people with a quarter of them on the dole. Efforts to support agriculture are not going well. St. John's merchants are sending their profits back to England rather than reinvesting in Newfoundland. It's a calamity if you ask me. On the other hand, I suspect they will squeeze the mining and paper companies to make up for lack of profit elsewhere. The whole situation is worrisome.

At my end, you'll be pleased to know I am close to signing contracts with a steel company out of Wilmington, Delaware. The American government is strongly considering lowering the tariff on fluorspar, which is the final piece to clinching the contract. I suspect they are looking at events unfolding in Europe and want to be ready in case of war.

I don't know if you hear anything at your end from the Brits, but this fellow Hitler is starting to rattle some nerves in the U.S. I'm certainly not in favor of another war, but you have to admit it would be good for business.

All the best to you and Urla,
Walter

St. Lawrence, Newfoundland

June 22, 1935

Dear Dorothy,

Thank you for all the news about Edward and home. I am so glad the Nutley Symphony Society has been resurrected and that you are a driving force behind it. Hooray for you!

It's a beautiful summer day here and the children are just finishing school for the year. As Barbara and I were out for a walk after lunch you could see them all heading home, some leaping into the air or skipping while others had their heads down, walking slowly home with an obvious poor report card. Our two will be doing that before we know it.

Their freedom will be short-lived as this town swings into summer. It is a busy time for men, women, and children alike. How goes the summer goes the winter because a good fishery and good haymaking will ensure a family can be fed and clothed for another year. Everyone is expected to help, right down to the smallest. They still seem to entertain themselves though and you can hear children's games go on until dark.

I had another "first" today in my continuing adventure, but not one I would recommend. Several people have suggested that a good dose of cod liver oil will help my tiredness, as it is full of vitamins A and D. So I went to visit Uncle Louis at the cod liver oil factory where he works as manager.

Oh my heavens what a stench! The oil is made by putting fresh cod livers in a barrel with seawater. It is left to ferment and the oil rises to the top where it is scooped off and bottled. At certain times of the year, schoolchildren come by the factory and get their cod liver oil on the way to school—right out of the barrel. Uncle Louis made me take mine right from the barrel this morning. I took that as a compliment that he thinks I'm tough enough to have it like the locals. I barely choked it down, but with him and Barbara watching

I really didn't have a choice. He gave me a bottle to take home. I think that deserves a care package from my sister containing Fannie Farmer cookies or a mocha iced cake to help wash down the cod liver oil. I will watch the Post in anticipation.

It was good to get out of there and back into the fresh air. Barbara has gotten used to the strangest smells, including the rotting capelin that is now dressing our garden. Thankfully, the red rose bush I planted last year is full of buds, so she will soon have that beautiful fragrance become part of her repertoire too. No one plants roses here. Partly that's because the flowers take space from vegetables. It may also be because the most beautiful, lightly scented, wild roses grow all over the place. With the right breeze you can sit outside and think you are in the New York Botanical Garden.

I'm sure your flower stories can make mine look paltry, so I will stop now. Barbara is waiting for dinner and we are both expecting Don home soon.

The mine is going great guns. For the first time since we arrived almost two years ago, Don is starting to look relaxed. Apparently, Siebert has found orders from the U.S. likely resulting from the talk of war in Europe. I find it so sad that we need a war to bring prosperity. So many people will be hurt and damaged forever and others will benefit. I simply can't think about it.

On that unsettled note, I will finish this and get it to the mail boat for tomorrow.

All my love to you three,
Urla

St. Lawrence, Newfoundland

July 4, 1935

Dear Mom and Pop,

Happy Fourth of July to you all! No holiday here for us, of course, and I've just come home for lunch. We have been so busy at the mine and the new mill that I have been getting home late every evening. Urla has been patient, but I thought I would not push my luck and came home early today.

She insists that we have Sunday afternoon together no matter if the mine is falling in on itself. We walk up behind our house a little ways and set up our picnic. I usually fish for trout in the little brook and Urla gathers handfuls of wildflowers. She has given up trying to teach me their names, so now she's working on Barbara, who frankly looks more interested in my fishing than the flowers. She is very much her Daddy's girl.

Urla is just putting Barbara down for a nap and then lying down herself. She has been getting more headaches than I remember but waves me off and says it's nothing. Now that school is out there are lots of young girls to come by and take Barbara for an afternoon walk, so that is helping Urla to rest.

I have sent two silver fox pelts home for Mom and Edith. I'm sure if Pop takes them into the city you can find a good furrier in the rag trade to make them into whatever you want. In fact, why not ask Sol Allan up the street? He is bound to have good contacts.

We have a new fellow in town and the young women have gone mad. The Commission Government has established a new police force for the outports called the Newfoundland Ranger Force. Robert Tilley is quite a handsome lad, tall and well built, but I'm not sure he could do much against any man in this town. They have a lot of duties, so we will see how is all goes. Mostly the young women are thrilled at the chance of a new dance partner!

ADELE POYNTER

Hope you are all enjoying a good day at the beach and old glory is flying high.

Love from Urla and me,
Donald

St. Lawrence, Newfoundland

July 31, 1935

Dear Mom, Pop, Howard, Vi, and Edith,

Don tells me you have been having a wonderful summer at Oak Beach. I can picture you all there with the sun on the water and the warm sand under your feet. I laugh at the memory of us trying to coax King into the ocean a couple of years ago and he having no part of it. I hope you're having better luck this year.

Barbara's first experience of a sandy beach couldn't be further from Oak Beach. There is a beautiful sheltered cove with a full sand beach just north of St. Lawrence. When the weather is warm and the women can steal a few hours from the never-ending work of summer, a group of them will come calling, children in tow, and off we go to Shoal Cove. Usually we get a ride in the back of the mine truck or someone's horse and wagon.

What a beautiful spot it is. The dunes are ringed by masses of blue and yellow irises and a river runs through them down to the sea. The water is very shallow and unbelievably cold. I've been in up to my knees, but when everything goes blue I figure it's time to get out!

We all settle in one area and out come blankets and picnics. The children usually wear underwear (not sure if anyone here has a bathing suit) and often keep their wool sweaters on top. They dash into the waves, scream with delight as the freezing water hits their white ankles, and run back up to their mothers. The women sit on rough old wool blankets, smoking or chatting with bandannas tied on their heads to keep the wind at bay. Barbara sits in amongst them all, *usually licking the molasses off someone's fresh bread, and kept entertained by watching everyone.*

It's a wonderful scene. I've decided that something about the beach makes people happy and it doesn't seem to matter what the temperature is. In fact, I'm starting to wonder whether they find the bracing water here more satisfying than we find Oak Beach. Or maybe these people simply find everything more satisfying.

My garden is coming along although slowly. At least I have learned my lesson not to plant anything with a long growing season. Don still kids me about last year's dwarf corn and green tomatoes. He says this year everything will come out in perfect size for Barbara, which I think is an insult to how big I can grow things! I hope to show him wrong.

So stay tuned for more garden news.

In the meantime, we send lots of love from our beach to yours.

As ever,
Urla

St. Lawrence, Newfoundland

August 17, 1935

Dear Ivah,

I was so happy to hear from you last week. Your trip to Sandy Hook with John and his parents sounded lovely. Is it as serious as it sounds? Do Mother and Daddy like him? I haven't heard anything about him from home, so that may be a good or bad thing! I hope you are happy, dear one.

The air is getting cooler here and I'm afraid that signals an early close to summer. I enjoyed a wonderful long walk this morning while Barbara was looked after by a neighbor girl. I was roaming the beach hoping to find a message in a bottle. I would dearly love to find one containing some classified military information or a lover's poem or an SOS. Maybe I'll prepare one myself and send it on its way.

No sooner was I thinking that when I came up on some dead creatures on the beach. There in front of me was a seal and a sheep on the same stretch—one thrown up from the sea and the other having fallen into it, meeting here in an incongruous fashion. Did they meet before they died? Exchange glances? Exchange pleas for help? Perhaps they comforted each other. I would love to know their story.

We have just finished supper and Don is home early tonight for a change. He is working so hard and thankfully has finished some long overdue improvements at the mine site. I don't like to talk to him about work too much, but it was truly awful that the men had no toilet facilities or change rooms. So that is some improvement.

Write me more about this special John when you can. Barbara sends her Aunt Vivi big delicious hugs, as do I.

Love,
Urla

St. Lawrence, Newfoundland

August 31, 1935

Dear Mom and Pop,

I realize my correspondence has been slow, but we are going full throttle with this operation while the weather is good and I have time for little else.

Turns out my salmon fishing trip at the end of July will have to be my only one for the year. Thankfully it was a fruitful one and, Pop, I can't wait to take you to the Cape Roger river. I caught a couple of twelve pound beauties, and on our last day we hit a run of smaller ones making their way to the head of the river. They gave quite the fight, but in the end we won. Urla was very pleased to have fresh salmon for a few days. By the way, Barbara now eats everything we do, with twice the appetite.

If Siebert can clinch the deal with the Wilmington steel companies I'm hoping for a raise and then I will treat myself to a new rod for next season.

I'm a little concerned about Urla's health. She is still getting headaches and the other night seemed quite lost during our regular game of bridge. She isn't worried and says it is just fatigue. That doc from the next community will be in town next week and I will get him to have a look at her. I know you sometimes see the Crammonds at church, but please don't mention anything to them. I don't want to alarm them unnecessarily.

Otherwise, we three are doing well. The fresh salt air agrees with Barbara and she is thriving. We can't wait for her to start talking as she is surrounded by children who say "tings" and "tink." You might have to get a translator for when we visit.

The mail boat is coming more often now, so you should receive this in jig time. Hope you all have a good last weekend at the beach.

As ever,
Donald

St. Lawrence, Newfoundland

September 1, 1935

Hello Mother,

Barbara and I are making jam today and it made me think of doing the same with you when I was little. I remember fresh raspberries and red currants and you straining the jelly through cheesecloth.

Our operation is a little rougher here and I have to admit that putting Barbara on quality control was probably not a good idea. We are making blueberry and partridgeberry jam with every berry picked by us, and a few twigs and leaves for good measure. Berry picking is a major affair here with the kids going with their pickers, older ones with their dippers, and adults with buckets and flour sacks.

I buy my bread from a neighbor since I simply can't make it like any woman in town. I can tell you there is no better taste than her warm bread, fresh butter, and our jam. I may send some home for Christmas so you can give me your opinion.

I wonder if you could look around my old bedroom for the scarf you gave me when we first left Brooklyn? I can't find it anywhere, so I may have it there. Please let me know as I am worried about it.

I'm glad you both like John, and I hope this one stays around longer then a month! Ivah seems very happy.

Love to you both,
Urla

                            St. Lawrence, Newfoundland

                                      September 12, 1935

Dear Ivah,

I had to quickly write you. I walked along the beach this morning and what do you think I found? A message in a bottle. My heart raced as I sat on a rock and opened it. Wouldn't you know it was my own message, sent a few weeks ago and now come right back to me. So much for it being found by a handsome Greek sailor.

Love,
Urla

St. Lawrence, Newfoundland

September 26, 1935

Dear Mom and Pop,

Thanks for continuing the subscription to the *Herald Tribune*. We have both enjoyed all the reading within. Coupled with our nightly radio broadcasts, we are becoming the town source for news. Events in Europe are looking worrisome, but I'm glad to hear Roosevelt's New Deal is finally showing results at home.

Pop's new office in Philadelphia sounds like the right move for the times. I guess it was there you met Dan Rayburn. He wrote me a peppy letter about new work opportunities in civil. I told him to keep me in the loop, but right now I'm up to my neck in mining engineering and couldn't be happier.

Urla has become a master plucker! Mrs. Annie Turpin came to her rescue when I brought home twenty-six partridge on the weekend. I joined a couple of local men and a visiting doctor for a few days on the barrens and we were rewarded handsomely. We had good weather too and spent long days covering the bogs and outcrops. Urla didn't look too pleased when I landed back at the house with a bag of birds under my arm. Now she has the trick for plucking and made a delicious stew yesterday.

I have an opportunity to hunt caribou in November. A hundred caribou licenses were issued to Americans last year and they have been coming here since 1904 to hunt. I would love to join a group and get my first caribou.

Our doctor friend gave Urla a good going over and can't find anything obvious to explain her symptoms. The big worry here is tuberculosis and Newfoundland has had a disproportionate number of cases. They just opened up a diagnostic lab in St. John's if we need it. But he checked out her lungs and they seemed clear to him. Hopefully it will resolve itself. She is being her normal stoic self about it all.

Barbara is thriving and we feel certain she will walk before her first birthday. She sends love to her grandparents.

Love to all from us,
Donald

245 Hillside Avenue
Nutley, New Jersey
October 12, 1935

Dear Urla,

Your father went into the drugstore very early this morning (in fact it was still dark out) so I have some free time for letter writing. He is working so hard still and they seem to have trouble attracting another pharmacist to work outside the city. All the new graduates want to be in the bright lights of New York.

On the other hand, Hoffman-La Roche is moving to a spot just outside Nutley. They will be producing thousands of medicines in that plant, so we will probably have lots of young families around the place then.

Dorothy and Bill were here over the weekend. Edward is walking, talking, and into everything. He is a charming little boy although he looks like Bill.

We commented that we hadn't heard much from you for the past six weeks. Dorothy mentioned something about headaches that I did not know you were experiencing. Your father will send something up to you to help as I imagine you have no access to drugs. I hope Donald is taking good care of you.

I am not sure what you are referring to when you say you left your scarf here. There is nothing in your room, but I will let you know if something turns up.

We are heading into the city on the weekend to hear the symphony and have dinner out. *Porgy and Bess* has just started its run on

Broadway, but I can't get your father interested in anything but orchestral music. At least he did not mention bringing Granny Crammond, so it should be a real treat.

Write soon with some news from your end. I do hope the headaches have subsided.

Love,
Mother

St. Lawrence, Newfoundland

October 30, 1935

Dear Mother and Dad,

Your letter arrived in good time, Mother. I hope you both enjoyed your concert and dinner in the city. I miss large orchestral works although I have surprised myself at how well the accordion sounds with the violin.

I don't remember asking you to look for my scarf, but maybe my handwriting was sloppy. You must remember all those poor marks on my report cards!

We have already had a light dusting of snow, so winter may well be coming early to us this year. Last week we dug the last of potatoes, carrots, and turnip from the Poynter garden! I'm so pleased with the fruits of our labors.

This week I attended my first "wake." There is no funeral home in town, so the dead are kept in their own home and everyone comes to pay their respects. This is no quiet reserved affair! There is music and laughter and storytelling with lots to eat, and more importantly, drink. Every now and then a group will fall to their knees and everyone recites prayers together, usually working their prayer beads like knitting needles. Children run about, except right around the deceased, and it feels very much like a celebration. Sometimes a two or three day celebration! Then the priest comes and the body is taken to the church for a final mass and burial.

I have to admit that at first I was shocked by the lack of solemnity. But before I knew it I had a drink in my hand, listening to a story about the deceased. Before long this kind of send-off felt very appropriate. Even though this person had spent his life in a small community with a small circle of friends doing very small things, this kind of a raucous send-off means his life did not look small in the end. I think it is a very beautiful way to leave this world.

My love to you both,
Urla

St. Lawrence, Newfoundland

November 5, 1935

Dear Ivah,

I was waiting for the Argyle yesterday. When it rounded the Cape, I almost burst with anticipation of your visit—your first visit to our corner of the world.

I fell into a heap when everything and everyone was unloaded and you weren't there. You couldn't have missed the boat, but what happened to you? You told me you would be here.

I have so many plans for us when you come. The boat arrives in the early afternoon, so I thought we would immediately head for the church to light a candle in thanks for your safe passage. School isn't out yet, so we can go watch the oldest students prepare for the upcoming concert. They are performing "Julius Caesar." The Sisters will be busy teaching, so you will have to wait to meet them. From there, we will hurry to catch the post office before it closes. Miss. Fewer will be anxious to put a face to your handwriting and I've already told her you would be visiting.

Then we have to hurry along and catch Mr. Louis before he eats an early dinner. We will have a glass of his homemade blueberry wine and hear a couple of stories before we pop into the telephone office to say hello to Kathleen or Florence. We won't stay long because Mrs. G won't hear tell of us not stopping in for tea and partridgeberry duff.

Then it's only two doors to our house where Don and Barbara will be waiting. He will likely be standing proudly next to his partridge stew.

Oh Ivah, I've been waiting for the Argyle to come around the Cape.

Love,
Urla

St. Lawrence Corporation Ltd.
St. Lawrence, Newfoundland

November 9, 1935

Dear Walter,

I trust you received my monthly report sent out last week.

I am requesting leave from the mine for about a month. I am concerned about Urla's health and would like to bring her to the U.S. for medical attention.

I have full confidence in Celestine Giovannini to oversee operations at the mine, and Louis Etchegary has good control on the mill. There should be no interruption in filling orders.

Please advise as soon as possible and I will make travel arrangements. I must mention I received my latest statement from the Wayne Bank. I see the raise we agreed to effective July 1 has not been put into effect. My expenses may well be increased now and I would appreciate it if you could rectify this.

Best regards,
Donald

St. Lawrence, Newfoundland

November 11, 1935

Dear Ivah,

Don won't let me go to greet the boat anymore. I am so worried that you will arrive without me here to guide you through the town. I don't want you to start your visit without your compass set properly. You see, dear Sis, that's what happened to me. Nothing looks it, but it's a very big town.

Don't be fooled by the obvious. In truth, I am ashamed of my apprehensions when we first arrived in St. Lawrence. How could my view of isolation be so distorted? How could I not have known that you can be poor and rich at the same time?

You see, behind the door of every small house is such an enormous amount of life. Every room holds legions of stories. Every person is twice their size when they pick up an instrument. At first, their talents will seem humble. And then it is you that is humbled. Every mother has raised ten million children. And outside, every path has been worn by a few hundred years of feet and hooves. When you are on the top of the Cape, it doesn't seem possible that the ocean can be that blue and that vast.

You will need my help to see this. It's a funny thing. You think you are in a small, isolated place. I felt like I had been placed inside a glass jar. Then I learned to take a step back so I could truly observe—observe and endure. Oh it was a glass jar all right, but somehow I found room to dance in there.

Please promise me you will go right to the church and have Father Thorne call for me. I couldn't bear the thought of you being here in my place without me.

Love,
Urla

245 Hillside Avenue
Nutley, New Jersey

November 9, 1935

Dear Donald,

Mrs. Crammond and I are quite concerned about Urla's health. We understand she's been suffering for quite some time and we would encourage you to bring her back to the United States for assessment. To be fair, we are not just encouraging.

We will leave it to you to arrange passage. Advise us as soon as this is done and I will make the necessary medical appointments.

Naturally we all hope this is nothing, but better to be safe. In any event, we will enjoy the company of the three of you for an unforeseen visit.

I await a timely response.

Best regards,
James Crammond

St. Lawrence, Newfoundland

November 22, 1935

Dear Mom and Pop,

All arrangements have been made and we will arrive in Brooklyn on December 4th early in the afternoon. You can follow the Furniss Line schedule as before.

I'm sorry you had a brusque encounter with the Crammonds. Urla's symptoms have been very vague and it was hard to know whether to make a big deal of them or not. Urla herself did not want anything said to worry her parents.

But things have been going downhill in the last couple of weeks. Yesterday I came home to find her crying and wondering why Barbara wasn't dressed for school. Her friends here have been wonderful support and someone is with her most of the time. She is frustrated, too, so we are all at a loss.

Siebert is not too pleased for me to be away, but we will definitely leave on the first. We will stay with the Crammonds.

I'm anxious to see you all.

Donald

1936

245 Hillside Avenue
Nutley, New Jersey

January 6, 1936

Dear Mrs. G,

Happy New Year to you and the whole Giovannini family. It was a delight to receive your Christmas card, as well as cards from the Etchegarys and Farrells, among others.

Urla and I are both quite touched by your concern.

Events went very quickly once we arrived in New York. Urla's headaches were getting much worse and she became unsettled and agitated that we were not going to be back to St. Lawrence in time for Christmas. The Crammonds had arranged for her to see a doctor here in Nutley, but he was not comfortable with any diagnosis so referred her to a neurologist in New York City. He, in turn, sent us to see an infectious disease specialist. Just before Christmas, we received a diagnosis of tubercular meningitis, or TB meningitis.

We are still adjusting to the news and there is much uncertainty over the outcome. It is a form of TB, not that common, that affects the brain more than the lungs. Unfortunately, it is hard to say when she became infected. Of course everyone here says this happened in

Newfoundland, and I really don't have the energy or enough of a case to argue anything else.

Tomorrow Urla will be admitted to a sanatorium about twenty minutes north of here. They specialize in the treatment of latent TB. It's a private affair, and costly, but has a good reputation and excellent care. At this stage they have no idea how long a stay will be required. I find it difficult to read between the lines and I'm not sure I can let myself be optimistic given the grim faces that seem to greet us everywhere.

We have decided that Barbara will stay here in the care of Urla's parents, with mine helping as they can. I will be returning to Newfoundland after Urla is settled in. Our hope is that after a few months, I will come back to get Urla and Barbara and bring them home to St. Lawrence.

The doctor says we will know more in a few weeks, so I will leave it there for now.

Christmas here was rather subdued as you might imagine, although Barbara kept us all in the Christmas spirit. She is a walking, talking rascal. You would smile to know that every time there was a knock on the door, Urla would shout out "mummers!" At first it was amusing, but her look of disappointment was heart breaking.

I'm anxious to get back as soon as I'm comfortable with Urla's arrangements. She feels I should be in St. Lawrence too. Of course she feels this is much ado about nothing. Then on other days she is so confused that she looks happy to rest and get away from us all.

I will send news of my travel plans and I hope I can stay with you until my family returns.

Best regards,
Don

Montclair, New Jersey

January 30, 1936

Dear Don,

I had a wonderful dream about us last night and it comforted me all morning. You were fishing and I was filling my arms with buttercups, wild daisies, and blue flag iris. Your broad smile was like sunlight breaking through clouds.

I am so tired of being here when I know you need me. I think Sister Mary Borgia might come to pick me up and bring me back to St. Lawrence with her. She knows how it feels to be confined and has promised to come get me.

You will be pleased to know that I am practicing some new songs for our next party. There is a wonderful radio program on in the afternoon. It's called The Kate Smith Matinee. She is a wonderful songstress and I particularly love "When the Moon Comes over the Mountain, Every Beam Brings a Dream, Dear, of You."

I love her voice and I can't wait for you to hear her.

I really don't like the food here, but Mother says I must clean my plate. I'm not sure I really like Mother either, but she is trying very hard to be nice.

The mail boat is coming, so I will get this off to you.

My love always,
Urla

Montclair, New Jersey

February 13, 1936

Dear Don,

I woke this morning feeling full of energy. It's a very pleasant day outside and the nurses say we will all be out for some fresh air. Some days they tell you that, but it never happens. Some days they say I slept through dinner and you know I would never do that, so I'm not always sure they are telling the truth.

I keep a packet of nasturtium seeds under my pillow and they are often missing. Someone has promised to take me to see Porgy and Bess, but no one has ever picked me up. Methinks that morals might be quite flexible in this upstanding Methodist institution.

I have decided that confinement is not at all like isolation. Confinement is always empty no matter what they do to fill it. Someone mentioned the possibility of me engaging in a craft afternoon. I can't imagine anything worse than sitting around with people I have nothing in common with making things that no one wants. Thankfully, reading is the only thing that takes my mind off my confinement, at least for a few hours.

Are you coming by today? Please bring me the crossword, a handkerchief, and some blueberry jam.

Love,
Urla

Montclair, New Jersey

February 20, 1936

Dear Don,

I'm hoping you will write soon and tell me if there is a war on. I hear people whispering, but it seems the news is not to be shared with us.

They finally moved me away from an older lady from Newark who is so dark and moody I couldn't stand it. She used to call me Pollyanna, which I don't think was meant as a compliment.

I've come to believe most people don't understand happiness. Nor do I believe that most people experience joy. I'm not sure I did either before the last couple of years. But I've learned a great secret and I'll share it with you if you keep it close: the trick to finding joy is to carry it with you even when life is not going according to plan. I see it so clearly now—even on the days when I'm not seeing anything so well.

Mother and Daddy came to visit on the weekend. They mentioned something about Barbara, but it wasn't clear what they meant. I think they are angry with you, but I pay no heed.

I realize they probably have never understood me, and maybe the same could be said about me understanding them.

I am so happy, darling, that you have always loved me in precisely the right way.

Sometimes when I have my eyes closed and my visitors think I'm asleep, I hear their enlightened analysis of my life. I hear how shameful it is that having been isolated in an impoverished corner of the world for the past couple of years, I am now isolated in this hospital. I hear about how much I missed. They act like you and I were running away from something when we went to Newfoundland. Little do they know that we were running TO something.

Let me know when my rose bushes are in bud. I want to be home in time for the blooms.

My love always,
Urla

EPILOGUE

OTHER THAN HIS own story, my father's letters are of interest because of the many other stories wrapped up in them. I felt these needed to be told too.

First and foremost, Dad's and Urla's story is also the early history of the fluorspar mine, the project that would occupy most of my father's working life.

The history of the fluorspar mines in St. Lawrence is ultimately one of tragedy. In the 1950s and 60s, many of the miners became ill and died with lung disease, caused by exposure to radiation in the St. Lawrence mines. But in the 30s and 40s, before lung disease was evident, the mines provided income and prosperity to the people of St. Lawrence. This was a period of rejuvenation for that part of Newfoundland.

Although fluorspar was first discovered in the St. Lawrence area in 1870, mining did not begin until 1933-1934, as described in this book. It continued well into the war years and beyond. The mines received another boost when the Korean War broke out and production continued unabated until 1958.

There have been several books written about lung disease in the St. Lawrence mines, including a Commission of Inquiry in the early 1970s. So I won't attempt to summarize the findings here. However, there are a few incontrovertible facts particularly relevant to the story.

One, working conditions at the St. Lawrence Corporation mine were deplorable in the beginning years. The operation was conducted on a shoestring and should probably have been sold several times to larger interests with deeper pockets. Conditions improved under my father's management, but it was still the type of environment that would not have been kind to its workers.

Secondly, it wasn't until 1945 that radioactivity was recognized to occur in non-uranium deposits (such as calcium fluoride). It would be another ten years, 1955, before it was determined that radon gas entered the St. Lawrence mine through the water, not the air. These discoveries were critical in connecting the high incidence of lung disease in St. Lawrence to the mine, and properly addressing the problem. But they happened over a period of twenty years, not overnight. Not long after the dots were connected, proper measures were put in place to mitigate the health effects. There has never, to my knowledge, ever been evidence of attempts to conceal knowledge or wrongdoing on the part of the mining company. It is sometimes comforting to suggest a conspiracy when tragedy strikes, particularly when it strikes hard working people without many employment options. As the daughter of a mine manager, I would like to think people did the best they could in the context of existing knowledge and resources.

Walter Siebert died unexpectedly in 1958 and his widow immediately set plans in place to sell the mine. All of this was happening at the same time the jigsaw pieces were fitting together on the effects of radioactivity on the miners. My father carried on for several years, filling orders from stockpiled ore and trying to find a buyer. Eventually ALCAN took over the mine in 1964.

Although my father went on to have a successful career as a civil engineer, nothing would ever match the period he spent at the St. Lawrence fluorspar mines. He started his young professional life and his young married life there. He gave thirty years to that project. My father remained resolutely American, but he also became a loyal, energetic, contributing member of the St. Lawrence community and ultimately married into a St. Lawrence family. Over the years, he lost many people he cared about. The tragedy of lung disease became his tragedy too.

Like many men of his generation, my father always believed in the power of a handshake. Unfortunately, that is all that existed between him and Siebert concerning the division of shares in the mining company. The promise of an equity position was never put in a formal contract. When Walt Seibert died precipitously, so did my father's claim to ownership rights. For thirty years he had accepted smaller compensation as manager in the anticipation of an equity position. During the Depression years, he had the added pressure of contributing to his family's financial obligations back in the United States. So in the end, my father didn't benefit monetarily, as he should have, from the mines. Moreover, he carried with him sadness over the loss of life, including his own precious Urla. I still suspect he would call those years the best years of his life.

Although no one knows for sure, it is highly likely that Urla contracted tuberculosis in Newfoundland. The incidence in Newfoundland at that time was much higher than in other countries and regions. By 1940, the TB rate in Newfoundland was thirteen times higher than in Canada. Among other things, this has been attributed to long periods of being indoors together in the winter where highly contagious diseases could run rampant. Although I have no confirmation of this, it appears that Urla had tubercular meningitis. This would account for her headaches and confusion, and ultimately her death. At that time, the United States did not have a policy of inoculating young people against the disease, so Urla would have come to Newfoundland with no protection.

I have no actual letters written from her while she was in the sanatorium in the United States. I'm glad I don't since I cannot imagine her pain at being separated from her beloved husband and daughter.

Their letters also told much about the community of St. Lawrence and the Dominion of Newfoundland. It begins with them falling in love with the landscape of Newfoundland. They were unprepared to have that happen, but it started on the voyage along the south coast and continued throughout both of their lives. Many of us are familiar with this pull—where the air, ocean, rocks, and trees of Newfoundland put a spell on the visitor and the love affair begins.

How different this would have been from the landscape they had left. Nutley was, and is, a bedroom community of New York City, located just across the Hudson River in northern New Jersey. It is flat, with straight tree-lined streets and a middle-to-upper middle class population. My father and his parents were born in Brooklyn. They followed a wave out of the city in the early 1900s to smaller towns more suitable for raising a family. Nutley was primarily Methodist, conservative, and its people were moving beyond their heritage to embrace the American dream.

Although St. Lawrence felt very Irish to my father and Urla, in fact its Irish ancestry had evolved into its own particular Newfoundland version. In addition to this Irish heritage, St. Lawrence was influenced by classically trained religious orders, Italian and Basque families, and the proximity of the French islands of Saint Pierre and Miquelon.

The church played a pivotal role in all Newfoundland communities. That role was exaggerated in the more isolated places, like St. Lawrence. One priest, Father Thorne, was a fixture there for forty years and was a man of many interests. His passion for soccer and music kept his parishioners at the leading edge of both. Equally important was the role of the Sisters of Mercy. Their high standards of education and their focus on literature and music encouraged the natural talents of the population.

All of this was secondary to providing spiritual leadership to the people of St. Lawrence. The result was, and is, a community united in faith, a characteristic that has served it well through all the tragedy that St. Lawrence has faced.

Although St. Lawrence had its own share of people on the dole during the Depression, it also had a population of entrepreneurial, hard-working people. As everywhere in Newfoundland, the strenuous work involved in fish harvesting and drying is testament to the strength of these men and women. Mining, especially in these conditions, was hardly for the faint of heart. More importantly, the people of St. Lawrence were risk takers. Every man who left the harbour on a fishing boat, went down in the mine, or transported liquor to the United States during prohibition took enormous risks in order to support his family. Every woman who planted a garden in such an unforgiving climate, laid fish out to dry, and gave birth year after year challenged fate.

Their letters also illustrate well the special relationship between St. Lawrence and the French islands of Saint Pierre and Miquelon. Smuggling was common, although never easy. Although we call the islands close, the journey there and back involved thirty-five miles in an open boat often in rough seas. Basic goods smuggled from the islands at much lower prices helped people survive during the Depression. The variety of goods possible from Saint Pierre added an element of luxury at a time when even staples were hard to come by. There's something satisfying to picture the people on that isolated coast enjoying fine French brandy and good pipe tobacco that likely would not have been available to even the rich merchants of St. John's.

Smuggling also highlights the irony that a fluorspar mine in a Dominion of Britain might not have been developed without the illegal ability to bring in machinery and equipment tariff free from small islands belonging to France.

The relationship between the two places was not just around smuggling. A shared religion meant there were plenty of marriages between people from Saint Pierre and people from the Burin peninsula. There were strong business ties during and after Prohibition. As always, soccer remained a unifying force.

But my favourite part of this story is that my father and his first wife found fellowship where they least expected it. They found themselves among people who experienced joy even when life was not going according to plan. They found themselves among people who worked hard to make their lives as rich as possible. That is a gift, one passed down to many Newfoundlanders. I'm so very happy that I count myself as one.

Adele Poynter was born and raised in Newfoundland but also has strong American family ties. After living in other countries, she returned to Newfoundland in the mid 80s where she has worked as a geologist and an economist. *Dancing in a Jar* is her first novel.